SPY CLUB BOOK ONE

THE START OF IT ALL

BOBBEE MELLOR

Grosvenor House
Publishing Limited

The right of Bobbee Mellor to be identified as the author of this
work has been asserted in accordance with Section 78
of the Copyright, Designs and Patents Act 1988

The book cover is copyright to Penny Nicholls

This book is published by
Grosvenor House Publishing Ltd
Link House
140 The Broadway, Tolworth, Surrey, KT6 7HT.
www.grosvenorhousepublishing.co.uk

A CIP record for this book
is available from the British Library

ISBN 978-1-83975-734-1

Introducing Four Unusual Cats

The story you are about to read is set in a small village in the middle of the English countryside. It concerns four cats who live in one of the houses in the village. They are very special cats as they are all Siamese, a superior and intelligent breed of cat – at least they like to think so. Four cats might seem like a lot but their owner, Ma, is very fond of cats. She got one, then another and then another, until she had four cats and that is when her husband, Pa, said, "That's enough!" So, there we are – four cats.

The biggest and oldest cat is Jake, a handsome, dark seal point, who is very intelligent and just a tad full of himself. He likes to think that he is the leader of this little gang, but this is not necessarily the case. Libby, a beautiful blue point, with piercing sapphire eyes, is actually the one in charge. She has the ability to make the others do as she wants without them even realising it, although she is quite capable of issuing orders and expecting them to jump to it! Ginny, the caramel point, is so light in colour that she could almost be white – she is a very pretty cat but, in truth, a bit of an airhead. The smallest and youngest of the four is Wesley – small not because he is still a kitten but because he just never seemed to finish growing. He's a sweet looking little lilac point, who's intelligent and full of common sense.

So, there we are, the four cats, living happily and comfortably with their two humans. The two young humans, Claire and

Peter, who had previously lived in the house, have both left home. Peter was at somewhere called Uni and rarely came home. Claire got married and moved to a village not too far away. She would often come round to see Ma and Pa, but she usually brought with her a quite large brown dog of unknown breeding called Brian, so the cats tended to keep out of the way when he was there. Not that Brian was vicious, quite the opposite. He was an over friendly dog with a tendency to give the cats big slobbery licks. Also, his conversation was not particularly exciting and, all in all, the cats found him, rather unkindly, an object of amusement to be looked down on and made a joke of.

So, at the start of our story life for the cats was generally good. They lived in a large, comfortable house where they were well fed and completely spoilt, which had a very large garden to wander safely around and two willing humans to attend to their every need. Absolute paradise. Or so you'd think. But it was not as perfect as it appeared to be.

What was the problem? Boredom! Jake felt the need for some excitement in his life. He was always complaining that nothing ever happened, there was nothing interesting to do, and that everything was always the same. Ginny usually kept quiet. For reasons which will become clear later on, she was quite satisfied with her life. Wesley agreed with Jake because Wesley always agreed with Jake. He was bigger and stronger than Wesley and not afraid to show it. Only Libby would sometimes stand up to Jake, and tell him to stop moaning and find something to do if he was that bored. When this happened there would be a little spat between Jake and Libby and then things would calm down until the next time.

Then, one day, something happened which put paid to any boredom and gave the four cats as much excitement as they could manage – and not a little danger.

Chapter One

It all started on a warm Monday morning in early July. The four cats were at the top of the garden, lounging in the shade of a large apple tree, when they saw Claire's car pull up and Claire getting out with the ever-enthusiastic Brian. He turned to look up the garden, saw the cats in the distance and immediately made a bee line for the little group. As one the four cats rose up and leapt into the apple tree. Their lack of welcome for him did nothing to dampen his enthusiasm – he was used to it.

It was clear as Brian got closer, that the dog had major news which he was dying to pass on. He slithered to a stop under the apple tree and, without bothering with any form of greeting, started to tell them the news he was holding inside.

"Guess what, you lot? Guess what?"

"You've found a brain," said Jake, rather nastily.

"No." Brian paused, not quite sure how to respond. He tended to take sarcasm seriously.

"Pity." Jake closed his eyes as if incredibly bored.

Brian paused for a moment then decided that he'd never understand Jake's jokes so he might as well not bother trying.

"No! No! We've had a burglary!" he burst out, unable to keep the thrilling news to himself a moment longer. Jake's eyes flew open and all four cats sat up a bit straighter.

"What?" said Libby, whose blue eyes were round and shocked. "Someone broke into your house? Did you get him?"

Brian looked a little abashed. "Well, no. It wasn't our house. It was the house three doors down. Deaf Sukey lives there. The burglars took jewellery and money and Sukey never even woke up."

"Deaf Sukey?" queried Wesley.

"Yes. She's a cat. Very old and very, very deaf. You can't really blame her for not hearing them," explained Brian. "The point is, I overheard the neighbours talking to a policeman and he said it was the third burglary in the village and there have been two other villages which have had three burglaries." Brian looked at the cats as if that explained everything.

"What do you think we can do about it?" asked Libby. "We don't even live there."

"But don't you see?" Brian was struggling to find the right words to rouse the cats' interest. "These burglars are doing the rounds of the villages. Your village might be next! It might be your house they burgle!"

"If they come near our house, they'll find four sets of very sharp claws showing them they're not welcome," said Libby in a no-nonsense voice.

Jake was looking thoughtful. "No, Brian's got a point," he said slowly, jumping down from the tree, followed by the other three cats.

Brian's amiable face glowed with pleasure at having got something right for once. "Yes. You've all got to be ready to see them off if they come."

"No, no." Jake was impatient, not only at Brian's feeble suggestion, but at the fact that the other three cats had clearly not caught on to the amazing possibilities the situation had opened up before them.

"Just think. They are quite likely to target this village and if we're clever we can be the ones to catch them."

The others gazed in utter astonishment at the now thoroughly excited cat. Libby spoke first. "What on earth are you on about? We're cats. Just what do you think we are going to do? Lie in wait and make a kittizen's arrest?"

Ginny and Wesley grinned at Libby's pun but Brian didn't get the joke and sat there with a blank look on his face. Jake was too excited to get annoyed with Libby for making fun of him.

"Yes, we're cats, which means we can go places and do things that humans can't. We've just got to approach the whole situation from the point of view of what we, as cats, can do." He was really urging them on now, keen to make them see the possibilities. "Look. We keep saying how nothing ever happens and now we've been handed the chance of some action and excitement on a plate."

"What if they don't come here?" said Libby, who was determined to keep all four paws firmly on the ground.

"Then we can't do anything." Jake shrugged. "But I bet they do. There are a lot of houses in this village where the people are wealthy. Just look at the cars they drive. They'll have the kind of things these burglars are after. How could they not come here?"

The other cats still looked a little unsure, but Jake's enthusiasm was catching and they were beginning to feel some of the excitement bubbling over in his voice.

Wesley brought them back down to reality. "But what exactly are we going to do? We don't know if or when they will come to the village and what could we do to stop them anyway? They come at night and you know that will cause us problems."

"We need to find out what has been happening in the villages which have been hit. We'll have to use our own way of investigating. Brian's village is the most important as that's the one with the most recent burglaries. We need to investigate that one first."

"And how do we do that? What do you suggest we do? Enlist Brian as a Private Detective?" Libby gave a sideways glance at Brian, who was looking rather concerned that he might be expected to do something beyond his capabilities.

"We'll have to get over there and check out the place," said Jake, not at all disheartened by the other three cats' lack of enthusiasm.

Wesley stared at him. "And how do we do that? Jump on a ninety-seven bus?"

"We don't have any buses here now," pointed out Ginny, who had taken Wesley's sarcastic suggestion seriously. "At least hardly any."

Jake tutted. "We don't need to catch a bus. One of us will go back with Claire."

The other three cats and Brian stared at him blankly. Eventually Libby said, with more than a touch of sarcasm in her voice, "Of course. We'll just wait by the car and she'll offer to give us a lift."

Wesley shook his head. "You're getting a bit carried away with this spying malarkey, Jake. Be sensible. There's only so much we can do. We're only cats."

Jake sighed theatrically. "I wish you wouldn't keep saying that. We don't have to limit ourselves because we're cats. We just have to think outside the box."

Brian looked puzzled. "What box? Who puts you in a box?"

Ginny sniffed. "It's just Jake trying to pretend he's some sort of intellectual. It means you have to look at the problem in a different way."

The other three cats all stared at Ginny looking a bit taken aback. It wasn't like Ginny to have such an understanding of complicated ideas.

"Quite right, Ginny," Jake finally managed to say. "And I know just how we're going to do it." The others all looked at him questioningly. "One of us has got to sneak into the car when the door is open and hide in the back footwell."

"How will they do that without being seen?" asked Libby reasonably. "Claire's not blind."

"Brian will cause a diversion as soon as Claire opens the car door for him."

Brian looked more than a little alarmed at this. "How do I do that?"

Jake sighed impatiently. "When Claire opens the door to the front passenger seat you move away from the car. While she's getting you to come back one of us will slip in quickly."

Looking a little happier, Brian said grudgingly, "I suppose I could do that. But it might make Claire cross."

"Of course you can do it!" snapped Jake. "Don't be so wet. And it will have to be Wesley who goes."

Wesley's eyes opened like saucers and he stared in horror at Jake. "Me?" he squeaked. "Why me? Why aren't you or Libby going? You'd be much better."

"Probably, but we're too big," responded Jake. "You're the only one small enough to slip through to the back of the car."

"But I shan't know what to do." Wesley had a feeling that he was beginning to sound like Brian.

"Yes you will. You're a quick witted, clever little thing and Brian will help." Jake knew the value of a well-placed bit of flattery.

Wesley wavered. He was torn between the feeling that he was totally ill equipped for such a challenge and a warm feeling close to pride at the praise Jake had so casually given him. He had never before said anything so complimentary about Wesley.

"When you get to Claire's," continued Jake, as if there had never been any suggestion that Wesley might not go, "you jump out of the car, run off and find out what you can about the burglaries. Then you appear back at Claire's house and she'll bring you back home."

Jake made it all sound so reasonable, so easy, but poor Wesley couldn't help feeling that there would be a lot more to it than Jake was implying.

"How do I find out about the burglaries? Pop along to the local police station?" Normally Wesley would never dare speak to Jake in such a flippant way, but desperation was making him bold. Brian was looking worried.

"There isn't a police station in the village." He looked as if he felt personally responsible for the lack of a police station.

"Shut up, Brian," said Jake, and Brian immediately shut up and lay down. "Of course you don't go to the police station. Find out which houses were broken into first. Then speak to any animals around those areas, especially cats who are allowed out at night."

Ma and Pa always made sure the Siamese were in at night, with doors and windows firmly shut. It was a system which caused great annoyance to the cats, especially Libby and Jake, who were bolder and more adventurous than the other two and would welcome the chance to go out and about at night, occasionally.

"Listen to the humans," continued Jake. "They'll be talking about the burglaries. Pick up what helpful bits of information you can."

Wesley was on the verge of asking which bits were the helpful bits, but wisely kept quiet. He would just have to think on his paws.

Just then they heard Claire calling Brian.

"That was quick," said Libby. "You usually stay much longer."

7

"She just brought something over for Ma. I don't think she was planning to stay." Brian was beginning to get butterflies at the thought of playing his part in the escape. Claire was busy and in a hurry, and he knew she'd be cross with him if he didn't do as he was told. Brian hated Claire being cross with him.

Jake could see the indecision on Brian's face and wisely decided that a mocking comment would be no help at all. In a coaxing voice he said, "Come on Brian, we're all relying on you and we know you won't let us down."

Brian looked suspiciously at Jake, who had so often made insulting remarks to him, but he looked perfectly sincere as he gazed at Brian. "Okay. Here goes. Are you ready, Wesley?"

Wesley gulped. He wanted to say no but he nodded, incapable of saying anything. Claire called again, an edge of impatience in her voice, and Brian ambled down the garden towards Claire's car with the four cats strolling casually behind.

Claire, who was busy chatting to Ma, absently opened the front passenger door for Brian to get in, but he sidestepped her and went over to sniff the dustbin, which had been put out by the driveway entrance that morning.

"Brian! What are you doing?" snapped Claire. "I haven't got time for this. Come here."

As she turned towards the dog, Wesley, quick as lightning, slipped into the car and into the footwell behind the front passenger seat. He waited to be found, with his heart pounding, sure that he must have been seen, but both women were focussed on the apparently disobedient dog and had no idea that the little cat was now half hidden under the front seat.

Seeing that the stowaway was now on board, Brian gave the dustbin a final theatrical sniff then made his way back to the car and jumped in. Claire slammed the door shut, kissed her mother goodbye and got in the car.

As she started the car and pulled away, she began a long lecture of complaint to Brian for his uncharacteristic behaviour, which was so unwelcome on this particular day, when she was so busy. This lasted until they were nearly home, but Brian bore it remarkably well. He was actually feeling quite pleased with himself for pulling off his part in the deception so successfully. He kept his eyes downcast as Claire scolded him but there was a contented little smile on his face, which he hid by burying his nose in his paws and looking suitably sorry.

Chapter Two

The journey to Claire's house took about ten minutes. As they were pulling into the village Brian murmured to Wesley, "Nearly there. Get ready."

When the car pulled up on Claire's driveway she got out and went round to let Brian out. Wesley, alert and poised to act in the back of the car, waited until Brian slowly started to get out. Then he shot over into the front seat and out of the door. Claire, who was surprised to see him, gazed in horror before making a grab for him. She was quick but not quick enough for speedy little Wesley, who disappeared under the car and out the other side.

"Wesley, what on earth are you doing here? Come back!" shouted Claire desperately. She gave chase, closely followed by Brian, but Wesley was already down the garden and jumping on the garden wall.

"Nice work, Brian," he called back. "See you later."

"Take care!" called Brian anxiously, as Wesley disappeared into the field behind Claire's garden and was lost from sight.

Claire was beside herself and rushed into the house to phone her mother. She sobbed as she explained what had happened. "He must have got into the car while I was getting Brian away from the dustbin. Oh Ma! I'm so sorry."

Ma was trying bravely to be calm. "Don't worry Claire. He'll probably come back when he's hungry." But secretly she was worried that the little cat might try to find his way home and get lost or hurt. She wondered if she'd ever see her sweet little Wesley again.

Meanwhile, her sweet little Wesley was busy wondering what he should do next. He had forgotten to find out from Brian where the burgled houses were, so he wandered rather aimlessly towards the neighbouring houses, which also bordered the fields, hoping to hear some human conversation or meet some helpful animals.

He found a rather overgrown path which ran between the side of the fields and the gardens. All of the houses looked very old and cottagey and the gardens, like Claire's, were quite small, much smaller than Wesley's own garden.

He was so busy looking at the houses and gardens for some sign of life that he was completely unaware of a figure moving stealthily towards him from the other end of the pathway. A sudden noise, like grumbling thunder, drew his attention away from the houses and into the face of a very large, very unfriendly looking dog.

"Well, what have we here?" snarled the dog. "An unwelcome little visitor. We'll have to do something about that." The dog then bared his teeth, saliva dripping from his fangs onto the ground.

Wesley suddenly thought of his friends at home who would never see him again and would never know what had happened to him. Would they miss him? Would they talk about him from time to time until his memory faded and they forgot about him? While having this mournful thought Wesley closed his eyes and waited for his certain fate.

He became aware of another, louder snarl and realised it was coming from behind him, not in front. Great! Two vicious dogs to argue over his corpse. He opened his eyes slightly and glanced sideways. To his utter amazement he saw Brian standing by his side. But not a Brian he had ever seen before. His hackles were up and he looked twice his usual size. His teeth were bared, and he was growling threateningly at the strange dog, who was looking more than a little surprised.

"Hop it Bozo or I'll pin you up against the wall and use you for a toothpick."

Neither Wesley nor the strange dog seemed to find this a funny thing to say. Brian looked quite capable of doing just as he said. The other dog looked uncertain. Living in the same village he and Brian knew one another, but the dog had never seen Brian look so fierce. In fact, he had often ridiculed Brian for being a wimp. But he didn't look like a wimp now. He looked like a very angry dog, who fully intended to carry out his threat.

The now much less vicious looking would-be attacker decided that it would be wise to leave with as much grace and self-respect as he could find. He backed off slowly, muttering, "Cat lover. I'll see you another time, wimp." Then turned and trotted off down the lane as casually as he could manage.

Wesley let out a long, relieved sigh and stared in amazement at Brian, who looked quite normal again now. It was almost as if the ruthless avenger had been a figment of Wesley's imagination.

"Thanks mate. Thanks a lot. You really saved my bacon."

Brian looked embarrassed. "Couldn't let that oaf hurt my little pal, could I?"

"He looked very put out when you called him a bozo," giggled Wesley.

"It's his name," responded Brian simply.

He and Wesley looked at each other for a moment and then both burst out laughing, easing the tension and making Wesley relax enough to wonder how Brian had managed to appear at the right moment to rescue him. Claire's garden was surrounded by walls and fences designed to keep the dog safely inside.

"How did you manage to get here? How did you get out of the garden?"

Brian looked half guilty and half pleased with himself. "There's a bit of the fence which can be pushed back and I jump over it and go exploring when Claire's not about. If she saw me doing it she'd mend it, so I have to be careful, but I thought I'd better keep an eye on you. Besides you don't know which houses to go to."

Wesley looked gratefully at the big, kind-hearted dog and felt ashamed at the number of times he and the other cats had made fun of him to his face and behind his back. There was obviously much more to Brian than appeared on the surface and he would make sure the other three knew that as soon as he got back home. However, for now, he had a job to do and not much time to do it.

"Come on, Brian old boy. Let's start investigating. Which way do we go?"

Brian nodded at a very small cottage two houses down from Claire's and the two friends made their way towards it in a companionable silence.

Chapter Three

Wesley and Brian made their way to Deaf Sukey's house. When they got there, they found the elderly cat asleep on a cushion in a wicker chair.

"Shall I go and wake her up?" whispered Wesley.

"No point." Brian was shaking his head. "She won't hear what you're saying and anyway, as I said, she slept through the burglary and …" He broke off suddenly as two ladies appeared at the back door of the house.

"I'd better keep out of sight," said Brian, nervously, "or they'll tell Claire I've been outside the garden." He lay down by the edge of the garden wall as Wesley, whose heart was beating wildly, jumped onto the wall and sat down.

The ladies appeared to be making their way to the small vegetable garden and, as they got closer, Wesley saw that one of them was holding a colander. Good! They must be coming to get some vegetables for lunch and would hopefully talk while picking them. He was close enough to hear what was being said but forgot that he wasn't invisible. One of the ladies, the one with the colander, looked at Wesley and said, "Where's that cat come from? I haven't seen him before."

The other lady also looked at Wesley, who was beginning to feel uncomfortable. "Me neither. Do you think we should get hold of it and see if anyone's lost a cat? It looks like an expensive animal."

Wesley felt distinctly alarmed. This mission seemed full to the brim with problems. He stood up ready to flee but then Colander Lady said, "No, leave it be. Cats are independent creatures. It'll find its way home. Which is more than my jewellery will."

Ears pricked, Wesley sat down again. This looked hopeful. The two women started talking about the burglary. Colander Lady was obviously very angry.

"I'm thinking of getting a dog," she said, "but it's a bit like closing the stable door after the horse has fled."

"Have the police no ideas?" asked her friend.

"Them!" Colander Lady humphed disgustedly. "Nine burglaries in all and they haven't a clue. The only thing they seem to think is that they wait a week before moving on to another village, but they've no idea where they'll go next. If they stay in this area, they've a choice of another five villages."

At last, a piece of useful information – it seemed as if the cats had a week at least in which to make their plans, if the burglars kept to their usual routine. Wesley was so thrilled to actually have a useful piece of information to take back that he almost missed another.

"... and said he saw two people getting into a car and driving out of the village," Colander Lady was saying. Wesley's heart sank. Who were they talking about? Had he missed a vital piece of information?

"What was he doing out and about at half past two in the morning?" Colander Lady's friend seemed more interested in the man's strange behaviour than the fact that he may well have seen the burglars!

"Dog's got tummy trouble. Had to take him for a walk," responded Colander Lady, whose colander was now full of the runner beans she'd been picking.

Wesley looked questioningly at Brian to see if he had any idea who the two ladies were discussing. Brian gave a slight nod and started to get up as the two ladies made their way back to the house, now discussing the slow progress of Colander Lady's spinach plants.

Wesley turned to Brian. "Where do we go now? Who was the man they were talking about?" Brian got up and shook himself.

"Jasper's owner, Mr. McMurty. Jasper's the one with tummy trouble. He ate a sponge cake Mrs Chambers had put on her windowsill to cool. She doesn't know it was Jasper – she thinks it was the Dudley twins. It's given Jasper the runs."

"Yuck!" Wesley made a face. He knew what having the runs was like! "We've got to go and see if we can find out anything from Mr McMurty."

Brian shook his head. "Forget Mr McMurty. Jasper's the one to see. Follow me."

Brian made his way to the end of the field and then skirted round the edge of a couple of gardens, as he was still keenly aware that Claire didn't know he was out.

As they reached the end of the second garden Wesley could see a large Golden Retriever lying in the garden, dozing. He only hoped this one was friendly. Brian noticed Wesley's worried look and said, "It's okay. He's a friend of mine. Lives with two cats. Used to them." Brian gave a low growl and the retriever's head immediately shot up.

"Brian, old boy. What are you doing here? Claire will go mad if she sees you out. Hello there. Who's this?"

"Mate of mine, Wesley, Claire's mum's cat."

Wesley and Jasper nodded at each other. Jasper frowned. "Long way from home, isn't he?"

Brian sought for the words to explain to his friend exactly what the cats were up to.

"Me and my three friends are going to catch the burglars," blurted out Wesley optimistically. Brian and Jasper looked at each other.

"I know," said Brian, "but you can't tell cats anything, especially his mate, Jake. It's all his idea."

Wesley felt that they ought to get on. Time was passing. "We understand you saw the burglars last night. Can you tell us anything that might help?"

"Not really," said Jasper regretfully. "It was dark and they were all in black and I was a bit… erm… distracted."

"What was the car like?" prompted Wesley.

"Small. Dark coloured. Dent in the passenger wing. Rusty. The dent that is."

"So, two men in a dented, small, dark coloured car," summed up Wesley.

"No!" said Jasper sharply.

"But that's what you just said." Wesley gazed at him in confusion.

"Never said two men. One was a woman."

"What! How do you know if they were all in black?"

Brian nodded knowledgably. "Nose. Jasper's nose never fails him. If he says one was a woman, one was a woman."

"And she was young." A voice came from the tree above. They all gazed up to see a black cat staring down at them.

"Didn't see you there," said Jasper. "One of my housemates, Sooty. This is Wesley, a friend of Brian's." Brian and Sooty, already acquainted, nodded at each other.

"Hi, Brian. Escaped the leash again?" laughed the black cat.

"Never mind that," said Wesley. "How do you know she was young? How young?"

"Saw her didn't I?" The black cat casually started washing a paw. "I was on the wall by the village cricket green when they came and got in the car. When she closed the door she took her hood off. I don't think he liked that. I heard him shout at her but she didn't put it back on. Typical stroppy teenager." The black cat laughed.

"What was she like to look at?" asked Wesley eagerly.

"Blonde. Long hair in a ponytail. Smokes. Saw her light up as they drove off. Bad habit smoking." She looked down at Jasper. "I saw you and Mr McMurty too." She grinned. "You shouldn't have eaten *all* the sponge cake."

Jasper looked embarrassed. "Never meant to. Just got carried away."

"Talking of getting carried away. We'd better get back," said Brian, who was clearly concerned about Claire catching him outside the garden and making her cross again. "Do you think you've got enough to satisfy Jake?" he added, looking at Wesley.

"Well, we've got quite a lot of useful information," said Wesley, looking thoughtful. "And to be honest, I've had enough. Let's go back and get Claire to take me home. Thanks for all your help you two. Hope you feel better soon, Jasper."

The four animals said goodbye and Brian and Wesley speedily made their way back to Claire's house. Wesley jumped quickly over the wall as Brian worked his way back through his secret escape route. He was definitely not the kind of dog the cats had always thought he was, mused Wesley.

As soon they got to the back door of the cottage Brian began to bark. Eventually a rather cross looking Claire came to the door.

"Brian, what's all this noise? You really are being... Wesley!" Claire's eyes opened wide.

The cross expression on her face instantly disappeared and was replaced by one of sheer relief.

"Oh, Wesley. Where have you been, you naughty boy?" She picked him up before he could disappear again and took him inside the house, followed by a relieved Brian. Shutting the door firmly, Claire put Wesley on the floor in the kitchen and went over to the phone.

"Ma, Wesley's come back. I've got him here in the kitchen."

Ma's jubilant voice came over the phone. "Oh, how wonderful. But I can't come and collect him because your father's out with the car and won't be back until late."

"I'll keep him until tomorrow, Ma, and bring him over then. I'm a bit busy at the moment. He'll be okay here. I can give him some of Brian's dog food tonight. It won't hurt him. Okay. See you tomorrow. Bye."

Wesley gazed at Claire in disbelief and horror. Not only was she not planning to take him home until tomorrow, when he needed to get what he'd learnt back to the others as soon as possible, but she was also intending to feed him dog food. DOG FOOD! In Wesley's mind Claire had almost sprouted horns and a tail. Something would have to be done!

While Claire put some earth in an old seed tray and water in a bowl for him, Wesley thought furiously. How could he get her to take him home NOW? He *must* get home while the information was still fresh in his mind.

He sat listening to the ticking of the kitchen clock. It was the only sound in the otherwise quiet kitchen. Instantly, an idea came to his mind. He started to yowl – long and loud as only a Siamese can. Brian looked rather surprised and Claire turned to him and said gently, "Oh Wesley, don't worry. You'll soon be home."

Twenty minutes later, when Wesley was still howling, the gentle tone had slipped from Claire's voice and she sounded distinctly fed up. "Wesley, for goodness sake. Stop making such a racket."

As the horrendous noise continued Claire picked Wesley up, took him through to the small study and shut him in. A moment later his bowl of water and litter box were dumped inside with him. Not allowing himself to be dismayed Wesley upped the volume. For another ten minutes he howled at the top of his voice, wondering how much longer he would be able to keep it up.

Suddenly, from outside the door Wesley heard the sound of a long mournful howl. Good old Brian. He was joining in and the two of them were making the most awful din.

Ten minutes later Claire cracked. She went to the phone and rang her mother. "I'm bringing him home now. He's been howling and making the most awful racket ever since I last spoke to you and now my daft dog is joining in. I can't stand it any longer."

Ma's puzzled voice came over the line. "Wesley? Howling? He's never done that before. He's not hurt, is he?"

"He looks fine," said Claire shortly. "And he's definitely howling now. I'll be over in twenty minutes." Then she put the phone down.

She found a large cardboard box and pushed Wesley unceremoniously inside before he could try to wriggle away. Not that he had any intention of doing any such thing, of course. Claire dumped the box on the back seat of the car and opened the front passenger door for Brian. "Not that you deserve to come, you stupid dog."

Even though Claire was very cross with him that didn't dampen Brian's jubilation at the success of the whole plan – a plan with which he had helped. For the first time in his life, he felt a great sense of achievement. He gave a contented little woof and then heard a muffled voice from the box say, "Well done mate. You were brill." Brian put his head on his paws and felt that life was very good.

Chapter Four

When they arrived at Ma's house Claire's bad temper seemed to have disappeared. She got out of the car calling to Brian affectionately, "Come on you silly old thing. Have a run in the garden for five minutes, while I return this pesky little cat." She picked up the box from the back seat, by which time Ma had come out and was holding out her arms to take her beloved cat.

"Wesley you naughty boy. What did you think you were doing?" She took him out of the box and gave him a big cuddle. Then she put him down and said, "Go and find the others. I expect they wondered where you were."

Wesley and Brian scampered up the garden to where the other three cats were waiting impatiently.

"Those two seem to have made friends," said Ma, smiling.

"I'm not surprised," replied Claire, rather acidly. "They're both completely cracked." Then she and her mother laughed and watched as the two rascals reached the waiting group of cats.

"While you're here, come and see my plans for the Summer Show," said Ma and then the two women went inside.

The three waiting cats didn't exactly greet Wesley as a returning hero, but were certainly eager to find out what he had to say.

"Well?" said Jake impatiently. "What have you found out?"

Before Wesley could say anything, they heard Claire calling Brian. The dog slowly and unwillingly got to his feet. He would have given anything to stay but he didn't dare make Claire angry again. He said a reluctant goodbye and turned to go. Wesley rushed up to him and rubbed up against him.

"Thanks for everything, mate. I'll make sure the others know how much you helped."

Brian licked his head and Wesley managed not to grimace. Then Brian ran off towards Claire and Wesley went back to his housemates.

"What was that all about? Sucking up to wimpy Brian?" said Jake.

Wesley was a gentle natured cat but when he heard this he felt his temper rise. "If it wasn't for wimpy Brian I'd be dead!" he snapped, successfully silencing the snooty seal point.

Libby looked closely at the angry little cat and said gently, "Why don't you sit down and tell us all about it?" She patted the grass beside her and Wesley walked over to her and sat down.

By the time Wesley had finished telling them all that had happened, he was feeling very tired. However, the response of the three listeners was everything he could have hoped for and more. When he described his confrontation with Bozo, all the more effective because he made no effort to overdramatize what had happened, his little audience sat with eyes wide and mouths open.

Eventually Ginny said, "Brian did all that?"

"Yes," said Wesley firmly. "And from now on we're going to involve him in all our plans. He's earned it."

Jake sat very straight and looked as if he were about to argue but Libby said quietly, in a voice that silenced them all, "I quite agree. There are obviously hidden depths to our friend Brian. And he put the safety of our Wesley over and above his own freedom and fear of Claire's anger. In future we'll treat him with a little more respect." Libby's voice clearly showed that there was to be no discussion about this and, after a moment or two, both Jake and Ginny nodded.

"I suppose it will be handy having a roving reporter," said Jake grinning, then they all relaxed and laughed at the thought of Brian with such a forceful job.

"Now," continued Jake. "We've got to look at the information Wesley and Brian managed to gather and think about how we're going to use it. If the burglars keep to their usual plan, we've got six days before they strike again."

"What happens if they go to a different village?" asked Wesley. "They might decide to stop before they get to us."

"If the girl is young then I bet the man is too, and the young can be very arrogant," said Jake, who could be rather arrogant himself sometimes. "They'll be feeling quite safe because they've been successful so far and the police have no leads to follow."

"I wonder," said Libby slowly and thoughtfully, "do you think they live in one of the villages? That way they'd be able to keep an eye on the progress of the police investigation. And they seem to know a lot about the people in the villages."

The other cats looked at Libby with amazed respect. None of them had thought of that possibility.

"They could do," said Jake. "We'll have to review all the young people in the village, especially young couples."

"What about the other villages?" Ginny asked. "How are we going to review the young people in them?"

"I don't know," Jake reluctantly admitted. "Obviously Brian and his friends can do their village."

"What about Max?" asked Libby. Max was Jake's older brother who lived with Ma's sister, a rather eccentric woman who had a smallholding on the edge of the next village. The cats, along with everyone who knew her, referred to her as Mad Mary, a name she was well aware of and secretly rather liked. She very occasionally came to visit Ma and generally brought Max with her. Wesley and the two girls always found it amusing to see how effortlessly Max managed to put Jake in his place.

Jake frowned. "I think he'd be willing to help but how will we be able to explain what we're doing to him? Mad Mary was only over last week so she isn't likely to be over again for a while."

"What about the telephone?" said Wesley helpfully.

"Yes of course," said Jake. "I'll just pop inside and give him a call."

He gave Wesley a 'what a stupid thing to say' look, but Ginny, realising what Wesley had meant, said, "But he's right. Ma and Mad Mary phone each other nearly every night. If one of us hangs around while Ma is on the phone, we can yell a quick message to Max to alert him. He always sits on Mad Mary's lap when she's speaking to Ma."

Jake looked unconvinced. Libby had clearly been thinking something over. "It might work if we rope in Sherpa." Sherpa lived next door with an elderly man called Arthur. "He wanders all over the place. He might be willing to take a message to Max and perhaps to cats in the other villages if he knows any. We've got time."

The others looked rather dubious. "Do you think he would?" asked Wesley. "We've not always been very nice to him," he added, looking pointedly at Jake. This was true. Sherpa had been one of a litter of farm cats and the Siamese, especially Jake, had always rather lorded it over him for his lowly birth.

To the surprise of the other three Ginny stood up and said, "Leave it to me. I'll speak to him."

"Why would he listen to you?" asked Jake, looking puzzled, but Wesley grinned and said in a sing song voice, "Ginny's got a boyfriend."

Ginny tossed her head and turned away, successfully hiding a self-satisfied smile. She made her way to a small gap in the hedge between their garden and Sherpa's and disappeared.

"Well, there's a surprise." Libby shook her head. "I didn't see that coming."

"How could she?" said Jake. "A common farm cat."

Wesley opened his eyes wide. "I should keep quiet about that if we want the 'common farm cat' to help us."

Jake thought about this for a moment and then nodded. "I suppose so. Anyway, she's got competition. He's always knocking about with April."

April was a pretty tortoiseshell who lived across the other side of The Green. She spent a lot of time with Sherpa, but Libby had noticed the way she always fluttered her eyelashes and looked coy whenever she was around Jake.

One of these days she'll flutter her eyelashes once too often thought Libby angrily, and I'll batter her one. Then it occurred to her that if Sherpa became involved in their plan, then April almost certainly wouldn't want to be left out. Rats, thought Libby. Why is nothing ever simple?

She gazed moodily down the garden and then sat up straight, eyes wide. To the amazement of them all Ginny was making her way back up the garden with a large grey tabby alongside her.

"Our Ginny's obviously got some clout there!" grinned Wesley, while Jake struggled to arrange a welcoming smile on his face.

"Hello there, Sherpa. Has Ginny explained the situation to you?" said Jake, in a rather forced pally tone of voice.

Sherpa opened his eyes wide, not at all taken in by Jake's apparent friendliness. "I think I get the idea," he said, looking Jake straight in the eye.

Libby decided to take control of the conversation before things got nasty.

"We want to catch these burglars. We've found out that it's likely to be a young couple, who might actually live in one of the villages. We need someone in each village to check out all the young people living there. We think our friend Brian will do his village and we're planning to ask Jake's brother, Max, to do his, but that leaves five other villages to be covered. We wondered if you'd made any contacts in the villages on your nightly wanderings."

By the time she'd finished Libby knew that she was gabbling. Sherpa's unblinking stare was nerve wracking.

After a pause Sherpa said, "I might have." Then there was a deathly silence.

Eventually Wesley said, "Look mate, I know we don't always get on but this is for the people of our villages. They're being ripped off."

Sherpa opened his eyes in mock surprise. "Is it really? I thought it was so Jake could show what a clever, important cat he is."

Upon hearing this, Jake stood up and his fur began to bush out. He hissed at Sherpa who started to retaliate. Before it could get nasty Ginny stood up and said, "Stop it boys. There are more important things right now."

To everyone's surprise Sherpa sat back down and Jake, believing that meant Sherpa had given in first, also sat down. However, Libby was beginning to wonder if this new arrangement was going to work if they were constantly going to have to break up spats between the two big cats.

Before anything else could start, she said, "Will you do it Sherpa? You're our only hope." She glared at Jake who had looked ready to argue and then looked questioningly at Sherpa. He looked quickly at Ginny, who gave a brief nod, and then said, "I suppose so. How long have I got?"

"To give us time to plan I suppose about four nights."

Sherpa thought for a minute and then nodded. "Okay. I'll see Mangy Tom tonight. He's a stray and wanders everywhere. I'll get him to see Fluffball and Barney. They'll cover their two villages. Fred and Lucy Locket can do theirs. The only one I haven't really got any contacts in is Great Longton. It's too far for me to go there often. We'll have to hope one of the four we're roping in to help will know someone. Probably Fluffball as she's the nearest." He paused and looked round to see if the others were satisfied with his suggestions. It was rather flattering to see them all listening intently. He continued, "I'll arrange to see them again on Wednesday night so they can let me know if they've found out anything. I'll come and see you on Thursday – just before lunch as I sleep late in the mornings if I've been out all night."

Without another word he turned to go. To the amazement of Libby and the two boys he rubbed his head against Ginny's as he passed and said, "See you, Girl."

"Hang on!" called out Libby. "Tell them they're probably looking for a girl in her late teens with longish blonde hair, who smokes and is probably quite sassy. We're only assuming the man is the same sort of age."

Sherpa didn't even turn around, he just nodded his head once and disappeared through the gap in the hedge.

Altogether, Jake, Libby and Wesley turned towards Ginny.

"What?" she said, although she knew quite well what was on their minds.

"A farm cat?" said Jake, looking at her as if she'd gone mad.

Ginny looked down her nose at him and said, "A handsome, strong, clever farm cat who could knock you into the middle of next week with one paw tied behind his back."

Before Jake could retaliate Wesley leapt up and shouted, "I'm starving. Let's go in and see what Ma's got us for tea."

It was touch and go for a second or two and then Jake said, "Okay. After tea we'll go over where we are and then we all need a good night's sleep. We've got work to do in the morning."

Just then Ma called from the house, "Come on you four. Your tea's been down for ages. Aren't you hungry?"

The cats all rushed inside and made short work of the food in their individual bowls. No one ever tried to take food from someone else's bowl unless they were invited to. Then they quickly discussed the progress of their plan. They all felt they had achieved quite a lot in one day. Wesley said it felt like a week since they'd first heard of the burglaries as so much had happened – especially to him!

From the conversation they heard between Ma and Pa it was clear that Ma was not planning to talk to Mad Mary until the following evening, so trying to get a message to Max would have to wait until then.

All feeling very tired, they settled down on their beds and slept deeply until the morning. All except Wesley, who, in the middle of the night, had a terrible dream in which he relived his meeting with Bozo – without the happy arrival of Brian. He woke in a panic, his heart beating madly, and it was sometime before he felt able to close his eyes again. Eventually, he drifted off to sleep and slept dreamlessly for the rest of the night.

Chapter Five

The following morning the cats were awake bright and early and pestering Ma for their breakfast. As she opened two tins of very expensive cat food Pa, eating his breakfast at the kitchen table, said, "You spoil those cats." But he was smiling as he said it.

Ma smiled back. "Yes, I know. Who cares?"

Just as she finished putting the cats' food out the phone rang. Fate was about to be very kind to the four adventurers.

Pa started to get up to answer the phone, but Ma pushed him gently back down in his seat. "Finish your breakfast. I'll get it." She picked up the receiver and recited their phone number. Someone spoke and Ma's reply made the cats forget their breakfast and prick up their ears.

"Yes, of course you can Mary. Stay for lunch… Oh, bring him along. He'll be alright with our four… Yes, yes, okay. See you about ten."

Ma put the phone down and turned to Pa. "Mary wants to go over the arrangements for the Summer Show, so she's coming over this morning and staying for lunch. I'd better see what I've got in the larder."

"I suppose she's bringing that mad cat of hers?" said Pa in a longsuffering voice.

"It's not the cat that's mad!" said Ma with a grin. "Living with Mary would send anyone round the bend, human or animal, and yes, he's coming."

She turned to the cats, "So you lot better behave yourselves."

The cats looked at each other jubilantly. Now they could have a proper talk with Max and explain what was happening and what they wanted him to do. Things couldn't have turned out better. They hurriedly finished their breakfasts and then stood by the back door for Ma to open it for them. Once outside they made their way to their favourite place under the apple tree and settled down.

"So, what now?" asked Libby.

Jake thought for a minute and then said, "As far as the other villages go, we'll have to leave them to Sherpa and his mates for the moment. We need to look around here and see if there are any likely candidates for our two young thieves."

"How do we go about that?" asked Ginny. "Are we going to split up and go in four different directions? And how exactly do we find out if there are any teenage girls who fit the description Jasper and Sooty gave?"

Libby frowned. "I think we'd be better off going in pairs. Ginny and I will go together and you two boys can pair up. As to finding out what we need to know, we'll take a leaf out of young Wesley's book and ask any animals we meet. We know a lot of them anyway. It won't take us long because we know all the people around our part of the village. It's only the houses on the outskirts we'll need to check."

"It'll have to wait until this afternoon," said Jake. "Max will be here soon and we need to talk to him. Besides which, Ma won't be happy if we disappear and leave him on his own. We don't really want to draw attention to the fact that we've gone off wandering. You know she doesn't like it if we're away too long."

There was a general murmur of agreement and then silence fell. The sun was getting hot again and the cats began to doze in the warmth.

Sometime later they were woken by the sound of rattling and clanking, and they waited expectantly for Mad Mary's old Land Rover to turn into Ma and Pa's driveway. Everyone, including the cats, had been expecting the vehicle to give up the ghost for the past two years, but it always seemed to soldier on. The driver's door creaked as Mad Mary opened it and she got out with Max in her arms. He always travelled on her lap. Ma kept on telling her sister it wasn't safe but her warnings fell on deaf ears. Fortunately, Mad Mary rarely went out in her car and never travelled very far. She also drove very slowly. The two-mile journey from her small holding to Ma's house would have taken her at least twenty-five minutes.

Having got herself and her cat safely out of the car, after giving Max a kiss on the head, she put him down and said in a doting voice, "Go and play, my darling. Don't worry, Mummy will be close by."

Ignoring her, Max stretched slowly and deliberately and then stalked down the garden towards the waiting cats. He was a regal seal point, like Jake but slightly bigger, and the cats were rather in awe of him. None of them would ever dare tease him about Mad Mary being his 'Mummy'.

As he approached, they all stood up, eagerly awaiting the chance to tell Max about their plans. Max was aware that the others were full to bursting with some sort of news, but he continued walking slowly and majestically towards the bottom of the garden.

When he finally reached them, he sat down slowly and looked from one to the other, finally fixing his gaze on Jake, who wriggled uncomfortably.

"Hello Max. Are you okay?"

Max looked surprised. "Why wouldn't I be?"

No one quite knew what to say to this and there was silence for what seemed like a very long time. Eventually, having made his point, Max relented and said, "Well come on. What are you all dying to tell me? Out with it."

Jake looked at the other three cats and shrugged slightly. There was never hiding anything from Max.

"We're going to catch the burglars!" he blurted out.

"I see," said Max in a kindly tone of voice. "And how do you propose to do that?"

"Um, er, well…" Jake found it difficult to explain to his big brother, with Max staring at him, in obvious amusement.

Libby decided she'd better take over the explanation before Jake became a total gabbling wreck. She took a deep breath. "You know about the burglaries then?"

Max nodded. "Of course. Mangy Tom told me."

"The stray?" said Wesley, remembering Sherpa's mention of the wandering cat. "You know him?" Somehow, he couldn't see Max hobnobbing with a scruffy stray called Mangy Tom.

"Yes, indeed. Not the smartest looking cat but has brains."
Max nodded. "He comes to the small holding now and again
for a meal. He knows he'll always get something good from
Mad Mary."

To the cats' relief Max never referred to his owner as 'Mummy'
but used the name she was known by generally.

Libby took another deep breath and then continued. "Just
listen Max and I'll explain everything and then we'll tell you
what we want you to do."

Max looked a little surprised at the fact that they were going
to tell him to do anything, but he slowly lay down and looked
expectantly at Libby. She thought for a moment and then gave
Max a concise account of the previous day's events. When she
spoke of Wesley's encounter with Bozo, Max looked at Wesley
with something very close to respect in his eyes.

"I admire you for continuing with your task after such
a nerve-wracking experience. Appearances are obviously
deceptive."

Wesley smiled and then stopped smiling as he realised that the
last comment was not as complimentary as he had first
thought.

When Libby had finished her account, the four cats looked at
Max and waited anxiously for his response. Max, well aware
of the value of suspense, paused for a moment or two and then
said, "You seem to have got yourselves remarkably well
organised in such a short space of time. I suppose you want me
to search out any blonde, smoking, teenage girls in Braybury?"

The four cats all gave a sigh of relief. Max's comments seemed
to give the seal of approval to their plans. "If you don't mind,"

said Libby. "If it's not too much trouble." *Why on earth did I say that* she thought. *What is it about this cat that makes us act like halfwits?*

Max smiled. "It won't take me any trouble at all."

Wesley frowned. "Aren't you going to do it? Not even to help save our villages from these burglars?"

Max's smile grew wider. "I don't need to go poking around. A girl matching the description you've given me has moved into a house on the edge of the village. It belongs to Old Joe Finnegan. I believe she's his granddaughter."

Jake, forgetting to feel intimidated by Max, said, "Do you think Old Joe is her partner?"

"Hardly," responded Max. "He's crippled with arthritis. Besides, from what I gather, he's not very pleased to have her there. I was talking to Bruiser, his dog, the other day and he said she practically forced Old Joe to take her in. Bruiser doesn't like her. She kicked him when Old Joe wasn't looking. He'd have bitten her if he'd had any teeth left. Anyway, she sounds like a likely candidate for your teenage burglar."

The four cats looked at each other gleefully. They were making progress.

"What about her partner?" said Ginny. "Is there anyone else living in Old Joe's house?"

Max frowned. "Not as far as I'm aware. I'll have another chat with Bruiser as soon as I can. See what else he can tell us."

"How will you get the information back to us?" asked Libby. "You'd never be able to get here and back without Mad Mary getting herself worked up."

Max thought for a minute. "What about your friend, Sherpa? Could he come over for a chat in a day or so? I would send Mangy Tom, but I never know when I'm going to see him."

"I'll ask Sherpa," said Ginny, never doubting she could get the tabby to do anything she wanted.

"Well, that all seems to be settled." Max looked round at the other four cats. "You all seem to have a knack at this spying game. By the time you've finished roping in half the cats in the area, you'll have a proper little club."

"A spy club," said Wesley, giggling weakly. Jake looked thoughtful.

"You may be right. I'm sure there are lots of things we can help with."

"Jake. Let's just get through this first, before we start trying to compete with the Secret Service," said Libby, half amused at Jake's enthusiasm and half worried that he was serious. "The only problem now is that Sherpa has got all his pals looking for a teenage girl and it looks like we've found her. Now we need to find her partner."

Ginny shook her head. "No problem. Sherps will have told them everything. They'll be looking for the man and the car as well."

Libby nodded. "Good. That means we've only got our bit of investigating to do this afternoon and then we just have to wait for the reports to come in."

Having covered everything they could think of, with regard to the burglaries, the five cats settled down to bask in the sun and make lazy conversation.

Before long, Mad Mary called to Max to come and get his lunch and the other four cats ambled down with him to see if there was any chance of a snack for them. They usually only had a morning and evening meal but, on this occasion, Ma found some treats for them so that they wouldn't feel left out. Then they all settled themselves on the wide kitchen window ledge to wait for Max and Mad Mary to leave.

Chapter Six

Ma and Mad Mary had obviously had a lot to discuss and it was nearly three o'clock when Mad Mary and Max finally took their leave. Once the old vehicle had pulled out of the drive and started crawling up the lane, the four cats made for the top of the garden and waited until they were sure Ma was busy. Then Libby and Ginny made off in one direction and Jake and Wesley in another. They didn't expect to be long as they each only had a small area of the village to check.

Sure enough, just after half past four, Jake and Wesley hopped over the back wall and settled under the apple tree to wait for the two girls. When they hadn't returned after the boys had waited some time, Jake and Wesley began to think excitedly that they must have found some useful information.

As time went on and the girls still didn't appear, they wondered where they could have got to. The village wasn't that big. By the time Ma called them in for their evening meal and the girls still hadn't returned, they were getting seriously worried, especially Wesley, who couldn't help thinking of his encounter with Bozo.

When the two boys walked into the house alone Ma looked at them with surprise. "Where are the girls?"

She went outside and called Ginny and Libby for several minutes, before going back inside to find Pa. He was in the small sitting room they called the snug, watching television when Ma walked in.

He took one look at her face and said, "What's the matter?"

Ma struggled to hold back the tears. "I can't find the girls. I haven't seen them since after lunch. The boys were under the apple tree earlier on and I assumed they were with them somewhere. But when I called them for their tea, only the boys came. I've called and called but there's no sign of them."

Without a word Pa got up, switched off the television and put his arm round Ma's shoulders. "Don't worry, we'll find them. They'll have found a warm spot somewhere and gone to sleep."

He led Ma out of the snug and into the kitchen where the boys were sitting anxiously, ignoring their tea.

"See, the boys know something's wrong."

Pa picked up his mobile phone from the table and put it in his pocket. "I'll go and have a look round the village. If they come back, give me a ring. I'll ring you if I find them." And with that he was gone. Ma looked after him affectionately. Pa might tease her about the cats but, really, he was almost as fond of them as she was.

Ma and the boys waited anxiously but no phone call came from Pa and no cats appeared at the door. Eventually Pa returned home, shaking his head as he walked in the door. "There's no sign of them," he said sadly.

"You don't think they've been stolen, do you?" said Ma frantically. Pa shrugged.

"It's getting dark now so there's nothing we can do until morning. I'll make us a cup of tea."

Pa made the tea that neither of them actually wanted and he and Ma sat drinking it in silence. Jake and Wesley both jumped on Ma's lap and sat squashed together trying to both give and receive comfort.

Eventually Pa insisted that he and Ma went to bed. After giving the two cats another quick cuddle Ma allowed herself to be taken upstairs.

Jake and Wesley sat on the window ledge willing the two girls to appear in the garden. "I wish I'd never thought of catching those horrid burglars," said Jake, miserably. Wesley looked at him sympathetically but said nothing.

Nobody in the house slept well that night and by five o'clock in the morning Ma was back downstairs making yet another cup of tea that nobody really wanted. Pa came down while she was pouring the tea and tried to persuade her to go back up to bed but she shook her head.

"I'll never sleep. I won't settle until I know what's happened to my girls."

The two humans sat in silence while the cats continued to watch out of the window for any sign of their friends.

At half past six Ma rather reluctantly opened the back door for Jake and Wesley to go out in the garden, but she kept a sharp eye on them.

As soon as they were outside Wesley made a beeline for the gap in the hedge. Ma watched him anxiously, but she could still see him wandering in the neighbour's garden so she didn't call him back. Wesley soon found what he was looking for – a grey tabby coat half hidden in a flower bed.

"Sherpa!" hissed Wesley. "Sherpa, wake up!"

Sherpa opened one eye. "What do you want squirt? Go away. I'm tired." He closed his eye again.

Undaunted, Wesley carried on. "Sherpa, Ginny's missing."

Both of Sherpa's eyes flew open. "What do you mean – missing?"

"She and Libby went searching the village for clues yesterday and they haven't come back. They've been gone all night."

Sherpa sat up. "What direction did they go in?" he asked.

"Over towards the church. Jake and I went the other way."

Sherpa got up, stretched and then headed for the back wall of the garden, calling back to Wesley, "I'll find them. You stay here. We don't want you getting lost as well."

Wesley heaved a sigh of relief and went back to his own garden, where Jake was waiting anxiously. "He's going to look for them." Wesley said and then looked down the garden towards the house, where he could see Ma watching them through the kitchen window. "Let's go closer to the house. Ma's worried that we'll disappear as well."

They found themselves a comfortable spot near the kitchen window, where Ma could see them clearly, and settled down to wait.

They sat in silence for what seemed like hours but just before ten o'clock Sherpa appeared in the garden. He looked for the cats in their usual place under the apple tree and then noticed them down by the house. He trotted down the garden and had hardly reached them before he began to speak.

"They're locked in a hut on the waste ground at the edge of the village. Some kids deliberately locked them in. I'll give them a good scratching if I ever find them."

"Are the girls okay?" asked Wesley anxiously.

"Yes, for now, but I don't know how we're going to get them out. I tried but it was too difficult. I think only a human will be able to manage it."

"Perhaps we can get Ma and Pa to follow us there," said Wesley hopefully.

Sherpa looked at him and said, "And how exactly do we do that?"

"You know, keep meowing and walking away." Wesley didn't really think that Jake and Sherpa would support his idea, but he was desperate to think of something to help the girls.

"I can't see it working," said Sherpa reluctantly, "but we've got to do something. They've got no food and water."

The three cats looked at each other hopelessly, at a loss as to how to help their friends. Time passed while they wracked their brains to think of a solution. Then suddenly, fate took a hand again.

Hearing a noise, they looked up to see Claire's car pulling into the driveway and, within seconds, Brian was tumbling out of the car and lolloping up the garden towards the apple tree.

"We're here!" yelled Wesley and the big dog skidded to a halt and made his way back down the garden to them.

"Gosh Brian. Are you a sight for sore eyes!" Wesley couldn't believe their luck. Just who they needed.

"Ma rang Claire," panted Brian, "and said Ginny and Libby were missing. What's happened to them?"

"Sherpa's found them," said Jake, feeling slightly amazed that he could so easily give credit to the lowly farm cat. "They're locked in a hut. We couldn't think how to get Ma and Pa to the hut, but now you're here it'll be easy."

Brian looked eager and blank at the same time. Before Jake or Sherpa could say anything impatient to him, Wesley stepped in and explained to Brian what he'd have to do.

"You'll have to run off. Ma, Pa and Claire will chase after you and you can lead them to the hut."

Brian looked panic stricken. "But Claire will be angry with me and I don't know where the hut is."

"Don't worry," said Wesley, soothingly. "Sherpa will guide you to the hut and once Claire realises that you've saved Ginny and Libby, she won't be angry anymore. She'll be proud of you."

Brian's eyes gleamed. "Proud of me?"

"Yes," Jake joined in, realising Wesley had hit upon the way to make Brian feel happy with what they wanted him to do. "You'll be the hero of the hour."

Brian sat mulling over what the two cats had said. However, Sherpa, feeling that Brian had dithered long enough, was impatient to get on.

"Come on Brian. I'll wait down the end of the lane by the road leading to the church. Get the humans' attention and then run like billy oh. Make sure you don't let them catch you but don't lose them." With that Sherpa set off down the drive.

"Go on, Brian. You can do it," encouraged Wesley. "Just think how brave you were with me."

Brian shook himself and then trotted to the back door of the house, where he started barking loudly. Claire appeared at the door.

"What's the matter Brian? Brian, where are you going? Come back here." Clare stared in dismay as Brian trotted down the drive and out of the entranceway. "Ma! Pa! Brian's running away."

Ma and Pa arrived at the door in time to see Brian disappear along the lane. All three set off hotfoot after the escaping dog.

Brian had caught sight of Sherpa and was now making his way past the church and towards the less inhabited part of the village. He suddenly had a memory of a programme he had watched with Claire about hunting dogs and decided to add a bit of drama to his act. He kept putting his nose to the ground and then setting off again at great speed.

"What are you doing?" asked Sherpa, highly amused.

"I'm pretending to track them," panted Brian, whose tongue was hanging out. He was beginning to get rather hot.

The two animals, with their accompanying humans, were beginning to attract attention from people out and about in the village. One old man tried to stop the dog but, fortunately, he was not agile enough and Brian swerved round him and carried on his way.

Suddenly Sherpa, running ahead, stopped and said quickly, "Brian, there's the hut over there. Go up to it and start pawing the door and barking." With that he disappeared into the undergrowth.

Following his orders Brian made his way to the hut barking loudly. Two little faces appeared at the dirty window, amazed expressions dawning as they saw who the dog was and realised that he had come to their rescue. Brian was pawing at the door and barking as Ma, Pa and Claire panted up behind him.

"What are you doing?" Claire said furiously. "Stop making that noise."

Brian, not completely sure that he'd done the right thing, shut up. Before anyone else could say anything, the air was filled with the yowling of two desperate and angry cats. Ma's eyes opened wide and she went to look in the window.

"It's Libby and Ginny. He's led us to Libby and Ginny. Oh, you wonderful dog." And she threw her arms round Brian's neck.

Claire looked in amazement at the dog she loved very much but had never credited with many brains. Brian looked anxiously back at her. She knelt down by him. "Good, clever boy. Special treats for you when we get home. I'm so proud of you."

Brian sighed with absolute bliss. She was proud of him – just as Wesley had said she would be.

Meanwhile, Pa was looking at the door of the hut. "Someone's jammed this door shut deliberately," he said angrily.

He pulled away the pieces of wood holding the door closed and wrenched the door open. Immediately the two cats, tired, hungry, thirsty and covered in cobwebs, tumbled out of the hut and ran to Ma, who managed to pick them both up, laughing and crying at the same time.

"Come on," said Pa, "let's get them home."

As he turned to go, he leant down and patted Brian. "Good boy. I wonder how you knew they were there. Well done." He took Libby from Ma and put her on his shoulder.

"Thank you, Brian," said Libby. Ginny, meanwhile, was looking over Ma's shoulder into the undergrowth where she could just about see a grey tabby face peering out. Sherpa winked at her and then disappeared. Ginny smiled to herself.

Chapter Seven

The return home of the three humans and three animals was chaotic to say the least. As soon as the back door was opened Jake and Wesley rushed out, going from person to person and back again. Ma and Pa put the wanderers down and the sound of yowling cats and a barking dog, all trying to talk at once, filled the air. Ma clapped her hands.

"For goodness sake calm down all of you. Come on Claire, let's get these animals fed. Libby and Ginny must be starving."

They all trooped into the kitchen and Ma put down the food while Libby and Ginny drank thirstily from their water bowl.

Ma then went to the fridge and took out a pack of meat – it was sirloin steak, meant for her and Pa's tea. She cut a sizable piece off and chopped it into pieces, which she then put in a bowl in front of an amazed Brian. He looked at her and she said, "Go on, eat it. You deserve it," and ten seconds later it was gone.

Claire tutted. "He'll be expecting that all the time now." Then she smiled and added indulgently, "You're right, though. He does deserve it. I just don't know how he did it, I really don't."

Pa turned to put the kettle on for yet another cup of tea, this one more welcome than the rest now that Libby and Ginny were safely home.

"Well, never mind how he did it. He did and they're home safe and sound. Come on, we all deserve a cup of tea after all that running and excitement."

He looked at Brian and gave him a quick wink. He was the only one who'd seen the grey tabby moving ahead of Brian all the way to the scrubland. In an attempt to make sense of what he'd seen, Pa persuaded himself that the dog had simply been chasing the cat and ended up at the hut through sheer luck. However, there was no way he'd take the shine off the dog's triumph. The poor animal was so often the butt of everyone's jokes, he deserved his moment in the limelight.

Brian, completely unaware that Pa was on to him, basked in everyone's wholehearted approval and praise for the first time in his life. Wesley looked at him and smiled. He was a good egg, was Brian, and proving to be a loyal friend.

While Ma, Pa and Claire sat drinking their tea, the animals trooped out into the garden and up to their favourite spot under the apple tree. No sooner had they settled down than Sherpa appeared through the gap in the hedge. Ginny went over to him and rubbed her head against his. "My hero!" she murmured.

Sherpa smiled but said generously, "It was a joint effort. We couldn't have done it without Brian."

The five cats looked at the rather embarrassed dog. Jake put his head to one side and said in amazed realisation, "Wesley's right. There are hidden depths to you. You carried off your part in the rescue brilliantly. They all think you're an amazing tracker dog now."

Brian wriggled uncomfortably. If dogs could blush, he would have been red from the ends of his ears to the tip of his tail. He simply wasn't used to praise, especially from Jake.

Sherpa grinned. "He played the part all right. Kept putting his nose to the ground as if picking up the scent."

All the cats laughed, but it was friendly, affectionate laughter. It was unlikely now that any of the cats would ever again laugh unkindly at Brian. They had realised his worth. Brian didn't really understand why things had changed. He was only glad that he now seemed to be accepted as a friend, rather than simply tolerated.

"Well now," said Jake, "do you girls feel like telling us everything that happened yesterday?"

Ginny and Libby looked at each other and nodded. "But we'll have to be quick," yawned Libby, "because neither of us slept much last night and we could both do with a good sleep."

Sherpa sighed. "Tell me about it. I managed about half an hour's sleep this morning before Wesley woke me up and sent me off on a rescue mission."

"Okay." Jake sat up and spoke briskly. "A quick summing up from the four of us and then we let these sleepyheads have a nap. Libby, you and Ginny first."

Libby looked at Ginny, who shrugged. "You do it." Libby nodded and started her account which turned out to be quite brief.

"We got to the edge of the village and had a scout around but the only animal we saw was Leo, you know, the ginger cat who lives just past the church. When we explained what we were doing he was keen to help but hadn't really anything to tell us. He couldn't think of anyone who fitted the description and hadn't seen a car like the one belonging to the burglars, but said he'd ask around and get back to us if he found out anything."

Libby paused and her face became taut with anger. "After he'd left us we'd passed these two boys. We saw them looking at us and giggling but didn't think anything of it. They came over to us and, before we realised what they were doing, they picked us up, chucked us in the hut and slammed the door shut. They just left us there."

All the animals muttered about youngsters who thought it was funny to be cruel to animals and Brian growled threateningly.

"Anyway," continued Libby, "what about you boys? Did you find out anything?"

Jake and Wesley both shook their heads. "It seems to me," said Jake, "that, wherever Old Joe's granddaughter's boyfriend is, he's not here. So, we're no further on."

"Well, you are really," pointed out Sherpa. "You've eliminated this village and you also know that it's a possible target."

Wesley looked at Jake questioningly. Jake nodded slightly, then said, looking at Sherpa, "What's with all the 'you'? Aren't you in this with us now?"

Ginny and Libby looked in amazement at Jake, who appeared to be inviting the 'farm cat' to join their 'club'. Then Ginny looked at Sherpa. "Go on, Sherps. We need your help. You can do things the rest of us can't, just like Brian."

Sherpa shrugged. "I suppose I could give you a hand for a couple of days," he said in a rather unenthusiastic tone of voice. But when the others weren't looking he winked at

Ginny and gave her a self-satisfied smirk. The farm cat obviously had his uses.

By now Libby and Ginny were finding it hard to keep their eyes open. Sherpa, ready for his own nap, said his goodbyes and disappeared through the gap in the hedge. Libby and Ginny curled up together and were both fast asleep in seconds. The two boys and Brian lay in the sun talking quietly about the burglaries and what they could possibly do next.

Brian said that he had never seen anyone who might be the male burglar or a car, like the one Jasper had described, in his village. He and Claire walked around the village twice a day and he would have noticed anything like that.

Jake suddenly thought of something he'd been meaning to ask Brian. "Where's Simon?" Simon was Claire's husband, who didn't seem to have been around for several days.

"Somewhere called Doo By, gone on business for a month. He wanted Claire to go over for a holiday for the last week but she doesn't know what to do with me." Brian sounded as if he felt personally responsible for Claire missing out on her holiday. Apparently, Simon's company were paying for the hotel and had agreed to pay for a flight for Claire as well. It really was a wonderful opportunity and Brian felt bad that she wouldn't go because of him.

"Come and stay here," said Wesley as if this was the obvious answer. Brian looked embarrassed.

"Claire said it would be too much trouble for Ma and Pa and you cats don't like me."

"We didn't *dislike* you," responded Wesley, sounding a bit embarrassed himself. "We just didn't know you very well.

Now we know you better we like you a lot, don't we Jake?" Jake nodded.

"Do you really?" Brian looked as if he had just been given the most wonderful present.

"'Course we do." Wesley couldn't help thinking how easily pleased Brian was. He felt ashamed again of how unkind they had been to the big dog, before they had all got involved in the plan to catch the burglars. "We'll have to try and think of a way to get Claire to go away and leave you here."

Nothing came immediately to mind so the three of them sat quietly until Libby and Ginny started to stir.

When they were fully awake Jake and Wesley told them about Claire and her holiday and they too, agreed that it would be good for Brian to come to stay, especially if he could be there when they finally took on the burglars.

Although it was much too soon for their tea the cats felt peckish and wondered if they could persuade Ma to give them a few treats. These were doled out very sparingly but, as today had been full of a whole mix of emotions, they thought she might be made to give in.

They all wandered down to the house and made their way into the kitchen where Ma and Claire were sitting at the kitchen table having what looked like a very serious discussion.

"I don't see why you can't go. You are being silly. Brian will be perfectly all right here. Look at them all. They get on perfectly well. When else would you get to stay in a five-star hotel in Dubai?"

The animals looked at each other hopefully. Amazingly, it sounded as if the two women were also discussing the holiday and Ma was encouraging Claire to go. They forgot all about the hoped for treats and sat down to listen to the progress of the conversation. It was clear that Claire was beginning to waver, especially when she looked at her dog sitting happily with the four cats.

"I suppose I could. Simon would be pleased. He's been trying to persuade me to go."

Ma went over to a drawer and took out a Yellow Pages which she gave to Claire. "Find the number for the airport and book yourself a flight. If you go on Saturday morning you'll have a week there with Simon. You can come over on Friday night and Pa will take you to the airport on Saturday morning."

Claire hesitated for a second or two and then opened the Yellow Pages. It was obvious that she had been dying to say yes.

Within ten minutes it was all sorted. Claire had a seat booked on the Saturday morning flight and she and Brian would be over on Friday. Sometimes, in spite of the problems they had come up against, it seemed as if, occasionally, fate was on the animals' side.

What didn't occur to any of them was that just a few days earlier the thought of Brian coming to stay for a whole week would have filled the cats with dismay, but now the animals could hardly believe their luck. They were jubilant and Brian looked as if he was in seventh heaven.

With all the arrangements made, Ma brewed a pot of tea and just as she and Claire sat down to drink it, Pa came into the kitchen. As he poured himself a cup of tea Claire told him excitedly of her plans. Ma smiled at them both and said,

"I told Claire you'd run her to the airport on Saturday." Pa nodded. "And Brian will be fine here." Pa nodded again.

"It's funny," said Claire. "I never thought your cats were that keen on Brian. They always seemed to run off when he came over."

Ma smiled. "It just took them time to get used to him. They seem fine now, don't they Pa?"

Pa looked at the little group of animals. "Oh yes. Thick as thieves," he said thoughtfully. He couldn't get the sight of Brian following Sherpa to the hut out of his mind, but he was a sensible man and didn't believe that animals could plan things together.

The animals in question were celebrating the fact that Brian could now be part of whatever plans they made regarding the burglars. Forgetting the treats they had hoped for, they went back outside to the apple tree to discuss the possibilities until it was time for Brian to leave.

It was quite late when Claire called him. The three humans had been discussing Claire's holiday and had forgotten the time. Once Claire and Brian had gone, Ma gave the cats their rather late tea and then they all settled down to sleep. It had been an eventful day, one way or another!

Chapter Eight

Thursday was another hot, sunny day. After eating their breakfast, the cats wandered up the garden to the apple tree and settled down in its shade to await events. There was nothing they could do except wait to see if any news came from their messengers.

Once or twice, impatient for something to happen, Jake and Wesley went over the garden wall into the field at the back to have a mooch around and to pass the time. But they didn't go far and in fact, they didn't have long to wait for some news. They had just returned from one of their explorations when Sherpa appeared through the gap in the hedge, looking rather bleary eyed.

"I've been out all night and need a sleep but I thought you'd want an update."

Libby smiled. "That's very good of you. Have you any news?"

Sherpa yawned. "I've spoken to Mangy Tom and he promised to go and see Fluffball and Barney straight away and get them to cover Little Longton and Middle Longton. He'll ask them what they can do about Great Longton as well. That's one of the villages where the burglars have already been. The other two are Garston and Avebury." Sherpa yawned again. "I spoke to Lucy Locket and Fred and they're both on board. Now I really must get some sleep. See you later."

He winked at Ginny, who smiled and said, "I'll walk over to your garden with you."

The other three cats watched as the tabby and his girlfriend sauntered to the gap in the hedge and disappeared. Libby shook her head. "I really should have noticed that those two were getting friendly, but I suppose I was distracted by the fact that he and April always seemed to be together. Where is the lovely April anyway? I haven't seen her for days."

"She's on holiday at the cattery," said Ginny gleefully, having heard Libby's comment as she appeared back in the garden.

All four cats managed to look horrified and satisfied at the same time. Horrified because they'd heard some horrible tales about life in a cattery and satisfied because they knew Ma and Pa would never ever put them in a cattery. When they went away Claire always came over every day to feed and look after the cats and, once or twice, Peter had come home to look after them. "Poor April!" They all thought, but not totally sincerely, especially Libby and Ginny who were both pleased that the flirty cat was out of the way.

They settled down to doze again but it wasn't long before they were interrupted once more. A large, rather scruffy looking black and white cat appeared on the back wall.

"I'm looking for Jake, Max's brother," he said, without so much as saying 'hello'.

Libby looked thoughtfully at him for a moment. "Mangy Tom I assume," she said eventually.

"At your service," said Mangy Tom, bowing his head.

Jake stood up. "I'm Jake. Have you got a message from Max?"

"Got messages from several cats. Gosh, I'm hungry." Mangy Tom replied, with more than a hint in his voice.

The boys and Ginny looked at him in surprise, but Libby understood that whatever news Tom had, it would be kept to himself until his hunger had been satisfied.

"Come with me. I'm sure Ma will find you something to eat." She led the scruffy cat down the garden and the other three followed slowly.

"Surely she won't take him in the house," said Ginny.

Sure enough, not knowing how Ma would feel about a scruffy stray called Mangy Tom in her clean kitchen, when Libby got to the back door she sat down and miaowed loudly. It wasn't long before Ma appeared at the door.

"What's up Libby?" she asked and then caught sight of Tom. "And who might you be?" Tom gave a low, rather pitiful meow. "Are you hungry? Never mind, I'll find you something to eat."

She went back into the kitchen and the cats could hear her talking to Pa.

"It's a stray Libby seems to have found. I'm just going to give him a bite to eat."

Pa came to the door and looked out. He stared at the black and white cat and then at Libby. He was beginning to find the cats' behaviour just a little bit unnerving. He went back inside and then Ma appeared with a dish of cat food which she placed in front of the stray. She waited until he'd started to eat and then went back inside.

The four Siamese cats watched as Tom polished off the plate of food in double quick time, then licked his lips and gave his face a quick wash. They waited impatiently for him to pass on whatever news he had; he soon gave up on the washing and said, "Let's move away from the house."

They led him back to the apple tree and all settled down. Then Jake said, "Well, what have you got to tell us?"

Tom started. "I spoke to Lucy and Barney and they'll have a good hunt round their villages, but I really came with a message from Max. He's been down for a word with Bruiser again and what he had to say might interest you." He paused and looked at the expectant and impatient faces looking back at him.

Eventually Libby said, "What did Bruiser tell him?"

Tom looked at her appreciatively. She was a very pretty cat.

"Well, for a start off that girl is a nasty little madam. Old Joe's afraid of her. She threatened him and, when Bruiser growled at her and tried to defend Old Joe, she told him to watch that his dog wasn't found dead in a ditch one day." He paused, fully appreciating the horrified expressions on the four cats' faces.

"Bruiser said she often goes out at night and doesn't get in until it's nearly light. He doesn't think she ever comes back with anything that might be stolen goods so the man must keep them. Bruiser's never seen the man but he's heard a car in the lane on the nights she goes out and she talks on her mobile phone a lot."

The four cats sat quietly thinking about what Mangy Tom had told them. They felt certain that Old Joe's granddaughter and her boyfriend were the burglars. They just had to find a way to prove it to the humans.

Tom got up and shook himself. "I'll be seeing Max again today as he'll keep checking with Bruiser. If anything comes up I'll pop back. It'll be nice to see you again." He was looking at Libby as he spoke. "You're a fine-looking cat."

Libby gazed at Tom with her mouth open wide, while Ginny and Wesley sniggered and Jake stiffened with indignation. Libby was his girl if she was anyone's.

Tom noticed Jake's look and added, "Don't worry. I haven't time for a girlfriend. Places to go, things to do." Then he looked again at Libby, winked at her and added, "But I might make an exception for you." Then he sauntered to the back wall, leapt over it and was lost from sight.

Ginny and Wesley were aching with laughter and eventually Libby and even Jake joined in. When he could speak Wesley gasped, "What a conquest you've made, Libby. Mangy Tom!" And that set them all off again.

When they had finally managed to stop laughing and become serious again, they discussed the news Mangy Tom had brought.

"The only way we're going to be able to expose these two is to catch them in the act," said Jake, "which means we've got to find out when and where the next burglaries are going to be and be there."

Libby nodded. "I understand that, but I can see one major problem. How do we get out of the house at night to be there?"

Jake dismissed this. "We'll work on that. There must be some way we can manage it. For now, we will have to assume the next burglary will take place on Sunday night, or rather in the early hours of Monday morning, if they keep to their routine. We've just got to find out which of the remaining villages is going to be next on the list. We'll have to hope that Bruiser finds out something for us."

Nothing else of interest happened during the morning, so the cats lay under the apple tree, glad of its shade in the hot sun. They went over what information they had and what plans they might make but, eventually, they all dozed off and lay fast asleep.

In the early afternoon Sherpa, looking refreshed and alert, came through the gap in the hedge and strolled over to the sleeping cats.

"Wake up, sleepy heads." He nudged Ginny and she woke up and rubbed her head against his. One by one the sleeping cats opened their eyes, stretched and sat down again.

"Any news?" enquired the tabby.

They told him of Mangy Tom's visit and Wesley tried to tell him of Tom's interest in Libby, but he laughed so much he couldn't finish what he was saying.

Eventually, Libby decided that she might as well tell Sherpa herself, because one of them almost certainly would. She simply said that Tom had evidently taken a fancy to her and said that she was a fine-looking cat.

Sherpa laughed with the others and then said, with a teasing look at Ginny, "And so you are a fine-looking cat." Ginny and

Jake both stiffened at his comment, but then Sherpa added, "Nearly as fine-looking as Ginny."

Everyone laughed and Jake and Ginny relaxed.

They all settled down to spend the rest of the day chatting quietly about events so far, completely unaware that Pa was standing by the kitchen window watching them thoughtfully. First Brian, now Sherpa. What was going on with those cats?

Chapter Nine

The cats woke up on Friday morning with a feeling of anticipation – Brian was coming to stay. They had a lot to tell him and might have more if Mangy Tom brought more news from Max. The others teased Libby about a possible visit from her new admirer and she took it all good naturedly.

After breakfast they made their way up to their usual spot and settled down to wait for any visitors. No one came in the morning and Jake and Wesley wandered off into the fields to pass some time. They met Leo, the cat who lived just by the church, and told him what they had learnt about the burglaries from Mangy Tom. Leo was very interested and said he'd be willing to help if they needed him. They thanked him and said they'd let him know. Then they went back to the garden to tell the girls about Leo's offer.

"Another one for Jake's Spy Club?" said Wesley cheekily, and earned himself a cuff around the ear. Only a gentle one though because, secretly, Jake rather liked the name.

In the early afternoon Sherpa appeared through the gap in the hedge and had hardly settled down with his friends before Mangy Tom appeared on the garden wall.

"Hello, darling," he said to an embarrassed Libby, then noticed the tabby cat. "Hello Sherpa. Didn't expect to find you here. Thought you always said this lot were a load of high and mighty snobs who thought they were too good for you."

Sherpa wriggled with embarrassment. Trust Mangy Tom to come out with something like that! Libby, however, came to his rescue.

"We are snobs, but we make room for some commoners amongst our friends."

Everyone laughed and the awkward moment passed.

"Any news, Tom?" asked Sherpa. "They've told me what Max found out yesterday."

"Well now," said Tom, clearly thrilled to be bringing some really important information. "You'd better get your skates on because the next burglary is going to be tomorrow night, not Sunday, and it's going to be here in Lower Barton."

The cats all started talking at once until Libby quietened them all with a loud yowl. "SILENCE!" Everyone immediately stopped talking, more from shock than obedience. "Let Tom finish what he has to say," she said, when they were all quiet. Then she remembered his demands the previous day. "Unless you want me to get Ma to give you something to eat?"

"Nice of you to offer," said Tom, "but I've just had a good feed at one of my stopping off points in the village. Mrs Leadbetter."

Clearly Tom had a regular group of people willing to give him a feed whenever he appeared at their houses. He waited until he was sure the cats were all listening and then told them what he had discovered.

"I called on Max just before lunchtime because I knew he meant to call on Bruiser first thing this morning. He'd told Bruiser to be on the watch for anything the girl did or said. Fortunately, Bruiser might be completely toothless and a bit short sighted, but his hearing is excellent. Also, the girl obviously felt safe talking on her phone in front of him. Her name's Melanie by the way. The boyfriend's called Gerry."

The others all looked at each other. Hearing the burglars' names suddenly seemed to make them more real.

"Where is he staying?" asked Libby.

"Still don't know and we probably won't find out because they're planning to head off to London after the next burglary."

Jake looked horrified. "So we've only got this one chance to get them?"

"'Fraid so." Mangy Tom didn't seem particularly concerned.

"Why are they stopping now?" asked Wesley. They had been so sure that the burglars would continue their custom of three burglaries in each village.

"They've got something going on in London. Some 'job' has come up and they've got to be there first thing next week. Someone in London seems to be giving the orders. Bruiser said they didn't seem to be very pleased to have their burgling spree in the villages cut short, but obviously have to do as ordered by the bigwig in London."

"Do you know which house they're planning to break into?" asked Libby. They needed as much information as they could get if they were going to succeed.

"No, but Bruiser heard Melanie say that the 'old girl' wouldn't give them any trouble if she woke up, if that's any help."

The cats looked at each other trying to think of elderly ladies who lived alone. "Mrs Beamish?" said Ginny.

Jake shook his head. "She's got a live-in carer now. I heard Ma telling Mad Mary last week."

"Mrs Tompkins, in that big house on the edge of the village?" suggested Libby.

Jake nodded. "I think she's the most likely candidate. They'll assume that someone living in a big house like that will have plenty of things worth stealing. And it's away from the main part of the village. We've got to assume it's her."

"But she's very old and very feeble." Soft hearted Wesley looked horrified. "They might give her a heart attack."

"Any idea what time?" asked Jake.

"Sorry, that's about all Bruiser could remember. Anyway, job completed so I'm off. Let me know how it goes."

Tom stretched and then made his way to the back wall saying, "Bye, beautiful," as he passed Libby, who shook her head.

"Cheeky thing."

Jake seemed to be lost in thought. "Penny for them?" said Sherpa, giving Jake a nudge, something he could never have imagined doing a few days ago.

"What?" Jake came to suddenly. "Oh, I was trying to think how we're going to manage this. We haven't got much time and only one chance to get it right."

A cloud of gloom settled over the little group. The whole thing suddenly seemed full of problems.

Eventually, little Wesley sat up and said briskly, "Come on you lot, buck up. We know a lot and I think we can have a good guess at the time."

Having got the others' attention, he went on. "Jasper and Sooty saw them leaving Garston about half past two in the morning so they must have got there about one thirty. I bet that's their usual time. In villages, everyone's usually been in bed and asleep for ages by then and it's still dark."

At Wesley's words everyone brightened up. "He's right," said Jake. "We need to plan to be there in time to catch them coming out of the house – so about two o'clock."

Suddenly they heard Ma calling them for their tea. "Is it really that late?" asked Libby. "Brian will be here soon. We can sort out all we know by bringing him up to date."

Sherpa said his goodbyes and promised to try to be with them early the following morning – they had a lot to talk about.

Chapter Ten

The cats stayed in the kitchen after tea, waiting for Brian and Claire to arrive. They didn't have long to wait. After they had had their tea, Pa left to go and collect them, while Ma washed up the tea things.

Pa arrived back with the two holidaymakers just as Ma had finished putting the tea things away. Claire was bubbling over with excitement and didn't stop talking as she went from the car to the kitchen, bringing in her two cases and all the things Brian would need for a week at Ma and Pa's. Brian was thrilled to actually be staying there, especially as it now seemed he was considered to be a welcome guest in the eyes of the cats.

The five animals waited until Ma and Pa took Claire into the sitting room and then the cats gave Brian an up-to-date account of all they had learnt since they had last seen him. Brian listened, half in amazement and half in horror.

"You mean we've only got until tomorrow night? We'll never do it! I'll never do it! I'm not good enough."

"Yes, we will," said Wesley. "Yes, you are. Remember Bozo."

A memory seemed to flit through Brian's mind.

"What is it?" asked Wesley, feeling rather concerned.

"I saw Bozo in the village yesterday," Brian grinned. "He turned and walked the other way, quite quickly."

The cats all laughed, especially Wesley.

"And this is the dog who says he's not good enough." Wesley thought about the moment Brian had appeared at his side just as Bozo was planning to attack him and he knew there was no one he would rather have at his side when they tackled this nasty pair of burglars.

"Well now," said Libby. "We need to plan exactly what we're going to do tomorrow. That's the most important thing to do."

"The most important thing to do is to work out how we're going to get out of the house at two o'clock in the morning." Ginny's tone said she didn't think they had much chance of managing this. Silence fell on the group. Ma was fanatical about making sure the cats were safely shut in before she went to bed.

"We could just make a noise so that Ma would come down to see what was wrong. Then we could make a fuss to go outside." Wesley didn't think the others would think this was a good idea. Neither did he. Libby immediately put her paw on the problem.

"Ma would come with us and, since she wouldn't know what we were doing, she would alert the burglars."

"Well, I think we need to sleep on it," said Ginny. "Maybe tomorrow we'll be able to come up with a workable plan."

The others agreed and they all settled on their beds. Claire had put Brian's bed on the opposite side of the kitchen which made him feel a bit left out. Libby looked at him and said kindly, "Why don't you drag your bed over here, Brian, next to ours? There's plenty of room."

Brian didn't need asking twice and eventually managed to manhandle his bed over to where the four cats were settled on their beds. Within ten minutes they were all fast asleep. All except Jake. He couldn't stop trying to work out how they were going to get out of the house without waking Ma and Pa. If they couldn't come up with a plan the only option was to let Sherpa and the other cats catch the burglars on their own. And there was no way Jake wanted that. It was *his* idea and he wanted to be in on it with all his housemates.

He lay wide eyed until he heard the clock strike midnight. He closed his eyes tightly in yet another attempt to go to sleep. He was just beginning to drift off when, suddenly, he had a blinding flash of inspiration. Pa's study! Of course, Pa's study!

"I know how to do it!" he thought jubilantly. "I know how to do it!"

Pa's study was a small room at the back of the house. Pa had used it whenever he worked from home. No one had been allowed in there without good reason – it was his sanctuary. Since his retirement a year ago he only used it to complete the odd bits of work he occasionally did for his old company and to do the accounts for a charity he supported. It was rarely used now and there was a good reason why Jake felt that Pa's study was the solution to their problem.

He wondered whether to wake the others to tell them his idea. He had just decided to let them sleep on and tell them in the morning when Libby stirred and opened one eye. She saw Jake sitting wide awake and knew that he had been worrying about how they would make their escape. She was just about to speak comfortingly to him when she saw the spark in his eye. Her heart started beating like a drum and her eyes opened wide.

"You've cracked it, haven't you? You've got a plan?"

Jake nodded and started to tell her how he thought they could do it. However, Libby stopped him. "Let's wake the others. They won't mind us waking them when they find out the reason."

After a few nudges the other three were gazing blearily at the two excited cats.

"What's up? What's up?" asked Wesley, immediately thinking something was wrong. Libby grinned.

"Jake's only gone and done it! He's thought of a way we can get out early tomorrow morning." She looked at Jake, inviting him to tell them of his plan.

"It's not a hundred per cent. We'll have to check in the morning but I think we'll be okay." The others shifted restlessly, waiting for Jake to get on and tell them. He looked round at the four eager faces and said, "Pa's study!" He stopped, assuming they would all have thought of the same thing he had. They all looked completely blank.

"The window will still be shut," said Wesley.

"Quite likely," Jake paused, "but not locked. You know how Ma and Claire are always going on at Pa for forgetting to lock it."

"I don't understand," Ginny frowned. "We still can't open it. The handle on the window is too stiff for us."

"Indeed, it is," smirked Jake. "But I bet it's not too stiff for Brian."

Everyone turned to gaze at Brian, who looked alarmed.

"You can use your mouth and pull the handle up," continued Jake. "We know how to open the door into the study and we can shut it behind us, so that Ma and Pa don't hear what we're doing."

Jake gazed in triumph at the other animals, who were gradually coming to see the possibilities of the plan.

"We're going to do it! We're going to do it!" sang Wesley, capering around the kitchen.

The others shushed him before he disturbed Ma and Pa, but they were all laughing jubilantly. It really seemed as if they'd solved their biggest problem. If only Pa hadn't suddenly taken it into his head to start locking his study window!

They all settled to sleep again, but, such was their excitement, that it was some time before they were all sleeping peacefully.

All except poor Brian, who lay awake for some time after the last cat had gone to sleep, wondering why he always seemed to be the one the success of an enterprise relied on. It was the one drawback of his newfound friendships. It never occurred to the modest Brian that he always succeeded because he was, in fact, a very capable dog!

Chapter Eleven

When Brian woke on Saturday morning the cats were sitting looking out of the kitchen window and Ma was getting breakfast for her, Pa and Claire. It was just after six. Claire had to be at the airport by half past seven.

As Ma laid out cereal bowls and put bacon on to cook, Claire came into the kitchen and sat down, trying hard to keep her excitement under control. Brian went over and put his head on her lap. She fondled his ears. "I will miss you, Brian. Be good for Ma, won't you?"

"He'll be fine," said Ma. "You just have a good time. Is Simon meeting you at the airport?"

"He'll be in a meeting but he's sending a car to take me to the hotel. A limousine." Claire's face was a picture of glee. "I can't imagine how much the hotel costs. I'm just glad the company is paying."

"Well, you make the most of it. Ring us when you get to the hotel and give our love to Simon."

Ma went to a drawer and took out an envelope, which she gave to Claire. "Here's a little something to buy yourself a spa treatment or anything else you fancy."

Claire's eyes filled with tears. "Oh, Ma! Thanks." The animals watched the two women hugging. How typically generous of Ma.

Pa came into the kitchen carrying Claire's cases and then the three of them sat down to eat their breakfast. It was too early to feed the animals, but Brian managed to get both Ma and Claire to give him a bit of bacon. He was very fond of bacon.

At half past six Claire gave Brian a big hug, kissed her mother and then Pa put her cases in the car and the two of them left for the airport. Ma cleared up the dishes and then gave the animals their breakfast.

Having eaten breakfast, for once the animals didn't make a beeline for the apple tree. They needed to check the study window, but they had to wait until Ma was out of the way. They knew that she would take a trip to the village shop sometime in the morning, as she always did on a Saturday. She was usually gone for about half an hour which should give them enough time to check the study window.

They tried to wait patiently but it was gone ten o'clock before Ma got her purse and shopping bag and left by the back door.

Before she shut the door she looked at the animals and said, "Are you sure you don't want to go out?"

The animals all stayed put, so Ma shrugged and then left, locking the door behind her. She knew she wouldn't be gone long so they would be fine until she got back.

The animals waited a few minutes until they were sure Ma had gone and then, pushing the kitchen door open, made their way along the corridor to Pa's study. Everyone was very quiet, hoping that they would find the window unlocked. The door to the study was shut but Jake reached up with his front paws, pulling the handle down so that the door swung open. The five animals trooped into the study and made for the window.

"Now, Brian," said Jake. "Put your teeth round the window handle and lift it gently. Just enough to see if the handle moves. Don't open it."

Brian went nervously up to the window and put his paws on the window ledge. He leant forward and slowly put his teeth round the handle.

As he started to lift all four cats held their breath. Was it going to work? Brian took his teeth off the handle and smiled unsurely at the cats. They all looked at the handle. It was an inch or so out of place. It was unlocked! The five animals exchanged triumphant looks and then Jake said, "Okay, Brian, shut it again." Once more, Brian put his teeth around the handle and, this time, pulled it down.

"Quick now!" urged Libby. "Let's get out of here and shut the door before Ma gets back."

They left the study, and then Brian was instructed to put his teeth round the door handle and pull the door shut. This he did without any hitches and then they all made their way back to the kitchen.

By the time Ma opened the back door and walked into the kitchen the animals were all sitting exactly where she had left them, looking as if they hadn't moved an inch. However, before Ma could put her shopping down to close the door, the animals were up and on their way out. She had hardly closed the door before they were up the garden and settling themselves under the apple tree.

They had only been there a few minutes when Sherpa appeared through the gap in the hedge.

"Where have you lot been? It's nearly afternoon. I've been over twice already. I thought you wanted to start early. I could have slept in."

For some reason Jake felt reluctant to boast about having found the solution to their biggest problem – not something which would have worried him before all this started. It seemed he had learnt a little modesty. He simply said, "We've found a way to get out tonight. We had to wait until Ma and Pa were both out so we could check if it would work."

"Jake thought of it," said Libby, feeling praise should go where it was due.

"And Brian did his part brilliantly," added loyal little Wesley.

Libby smiled at Brian. "He did indeed. So, now we've got that out of the way, we need to get our plans for tonight sorted out. Jake, you go over what we've planned. After all this whole thing was your idea."

Jake was perfectly willing to take the lead, he was beginning to feel a real sense of excitement. He cleared his throat importantly and then saw Sherpa smirking at him and felt silly.

"Okay. I think what we need to do is this."

Half an hour later the plans were made, and everyone knew what they were expected to do. The idea was to wait until the burglars got back to the car and then, stopping them from getting into the car, the animals would make as much noise as possible, in order to wake the humans and bring them out into the street. After that it would be up to them.

Sherpa, who was generally out most of the night anyway, would station himself outside the victim's house to wait for the burglars to appear. Coming from Max's village they would have to go right through the village to get to Mrs Tompkins' house and would probably park the car in the village.

The animals discussed the possibility of them parking outside Mrs Tomkins' house, but decided that it was unlikely as the car would stand out there more than in the village somewhere.

As soon as he had seen where they were parking the car Sherpa would let the others know, so that they could be waiting there when the burglars returned. Having done that, he would go back to the house and, as soon as he saw them leaving, he would join the rest of the cats at the car, to lie in wait for the unsuspecting couple.

Brian was instructed to wait by the driver's door and make sure that Gerry couldn't get into the car. They didn't want him driving away before the humans came on the scene. As usual, Brian was proud to be given an important job to do but panic stricken in case he messed it up.

"Do you think there'll be enough of us?" asked Ginny, sounding rather unsure.

"I was thinking about that," mused Jake. "Leo has already offered to help and Beelzebub probably would as well. He's often out at night."

Brian looked a little taken aback at the name, but Wesley laughed and said, "Beelzebub is the local vicar's cat. She's got a strange sense of humour. He is as black as a witch's cat and was a very badly behaved kitten. But he's okay now and I bet he'd love to join us. He's always ready for a bit of fun."

"I'll wander round and find him and Leo and explain what we want them to do," said Sherpa. "Assume they're on board. I'll tell them to wait by the church gate about one thirty. That seems a pretty central place for everyone to meet."

"We'll meet them there then." Jake was beginning to feel a little less excited and a little more nervous now that they were so close to the actual event. The little group of conspirators looked at each other, all of them wondering if they would be up to the challenges facing them. However, before anyone else could speak, a scruffy black and white shape appeared on the back wall.

"Hi, you lot. All sorted?" Mangy Tom jumped down and strolled over to sit down by the little group.

"Come and join us," said Jake, with more than a little sarcasm in his voice. Then he remembered how much they owed the stray and added in a more friendly tone, "We'll bring you up to date with what we're planning to do."

When Jake had finished going through their plans, Tom nodded his head. "Seems like a sound plan," he said approvingly. "Now let me add a bit. I saw Sooty and Patch last night – you know, Jasper's housemates."

Brian and Wesley nodded.

"Anyway, they said they'd make their way over here tonight and lend a hand. They'll be here about midnight. They'll look round the village and get their bearings and then, luckily, they plan to wait for you at the church, so they'll meet up with your two mates there."

"That gives us two extra voices," said Sherpa. "It should be enough. Humans seem to wake up and complain when they hear just one cat meowing."

Mangy Tom got up, stretched and said, "I'm off for a snack at one of my regular stopovers." Then he added casually, "If I'm still around tonight, I might come over and join in." With that he hopped over the wall and disappeared.

Sherpa grinned. "He'll be there. I know him. He's dying to be part of it."

Jake mentally counted his 'team' and then said, "That makes ten cats and a dog. Between us we can make enough of a racket to raise everyone in all eight villages!"

They all laughed, then Libby said, "It might be a good idea to get some sleep now, because none of us is going to get much tonight."

Sherpa said he would go and alert Leo and Beelzebub and then go home to nap. He and Ginny rubbed faces and then he wandered down the garden and out of the front gateway. The four Siamese and Brian settled down under the apple tree and dozed on and off for the rest of the afternoon.

When they woke at teatime, they saw the car parked in the driveway and knew that Pa was home. He had obviously waited with Claire until she boarded her plane. They just hoped that he didn't get it into his head to go into his study and lock his window!

When Ma called them for tea, they wandered down the garden and into the kitchen, relieved to hear noises in the snug, which meant Pa was in there watching television.

Having eaten their tea Ma left the kitchen door open for them to go back out into the garden again. However, they all felt reluctant to leave the comfort and security of the kitchen. The seriousness of what they were doing loomed large and they were all experiencing butterflies to some extent.

At half past ten Ma came in to lock the door and then she and Pa went off to bed. Time seemed to go very slowly after that but none of them wanted to risk falling off to sleep. Eventually they settled by the kitchen window to wait for the clock to strike the half hour; one thirty – zero hour!

Chapter Twelve

For what seemed like forever Brian and the cats sat watching the minute hand on the clock move agonisingly slowly towards half past one. At twenty past Jake got up and said, "Come on. Ten minutes won't make any difference. Now keep quiet, we don't want to wake Ma and Pa."

The animals crept out into the corridor, Jake in the lead and Brian bringing up the rear. They could hear Pa snoring upstairs.

When they got to the study, Jake reached up and opened the door and they all crept quietly into the room. Jake gently pushed the door to but, as it shut, it gave a loud click. The sound of Pa's snoring stopped and the five animals froze. They waited in agonised suspense for two or three minutes. Then, to their great relief, Pa's snoring could be heard again and they all breathed out.

"Come on," Libby urged, "let's get going. Come on Brian, open the window."

Brian obediently went over to the window and took the handle in his mouth. He slowly lifted the handle until the window was nearly open. Then the handle stopped moving! Brian tried really hard but he couldn't make it move any further.

The cats held their breath as Brian took his teeth from the handle and moved back a little. Before anyone had a chance to speak, the dog put his head under the handle and pushed with all his might.

At first nothing happened but then, as Brian gave an extra hard push, the handle moved up and the window opened. The cats looked at each other in silent glee. Jake patted Brian and mouthed silently, "Brilliant. Well done."

He hopped onto the window ledge and pushed the window wide open. He motioned to the other three cats and, one by one, they jumped silently out of the window and onto the path outside. Then Jake nodded at Brian, who looked apprehensive. He thought he could get through the window okay – it was the 'in silence' bit which was making him pause.

"Go on, Brian. Just take your time," whispered Jake.

Brian took his courage in his paws and jumped onto the window ledge. His claws made a clicking noise on the wood and he held his breath. Then he stepped forward and jumped out. Even if his landing wasn't completely silent, it appeared to cause no problems. Jake could still hear Pa snoring upstairs.

Jake joined his friends and the five of them quietly made their way round the outside of the house, out of the gateway and down the lane to The Green. From there they turned left and made their way towards the church.

As they approached the church gateway, four dark shadows appeared on the churchyard wall and waited for them to arrive. Jake leapt onto the wall and into the churchyard, closely followed by all the other cats. Brian pushed his way through the swinging gate, which creaked slightly. Everyone listened to see if the noise had been heard but there was no disturbance and they all relaxed.

Jake and the others made their way to the church porch and they all crowded in. Jake jumped on the bench, which ran along the side of the porch, and addressed his little army in a whisper.

"Thanks, all of you, for being here. Let's hope we succeed in catching these two nasty young people. We'll wait here until Sherpa comes to tell us they have arrived in the village and where they've left the car. Then we'll all make our way as silently as possible and hide near the car. Sherpa will go back and watch until he sees them leaving the house. Then he'll slip back quickly and meet us there, ready to attack. Any questions?"

"Can't we stop them before they break in?" asked soft hearted Wesley. "If Mrs Tompkins wakes up, she'll be so frightened."

"Sorry, Wesley, they've got to be caught with the stolen goods on them. If we…" Jake broke off as they heard the churchyard gate creak. He was just thinking how unusually careless it was of Sherpa to come that way when he could easily and silently jump over the wall when, to everyone's amazement, they saw a spritely Jack Russell trotting up the pathway towards the church porch.

"Hello, you lot," he whispered. "What's going on?"

He looked round at the gawping faces looking back at him. Leo looked closely at him. "It's Toby, Mrs Whittacker's dog. He lives on The Green." He crept up to the little dog and whispered, "What are you doing here, Toby?"

"I've got a cat flap. Come and go as I please," he answered, as if that explained everything. The other animals looked at him rather bemused.

"And?" Jake interrupted. "What's that got to do with anything?"

"Saw you lot coming in here. Seemed to me like something was going on. Thought I'd see what it was. Wondered if I could help." The bright-eyed little dog looked round at them all eagerly. He was obviously dying to be included in whatever they were up to.

"One more won't hurt," said Libby. "Tell him what we're doing, Jake, but be quick."

Quickly and quietly Jake explained the plan and the Jack Russell's eyes gleamed with anticipation and excitement.

"Count me in," he said. "Been longing for a bit of excitement for ages."

He pushed his way into the rather crowded porch. Jake quickly introduced the others to Toby and everyone gave him a friendly nod.

"We're just waiting for Sherpa to come and give us the off," added Jake.

"Know Sherpa. Meet him out and about at night sometimes. Good lad. Solid. Trustworthy." Toby finished reciting his approval of Sherpa and settled down to wait with the rest.

Time seemed to pass very slowly. The only interruption was the arrival of a rather scruffy looking cat who casually positioned himself just outside the church porch. Having settled himself, Mangy Tom looked at the little Jack Russell and, turning to Wesley, hissed out of the side of his mouth, "Who's he?"

"New recruit," said Wesley, briefly. Tom nodded and then silence reigned again.

More minutes passed and then the animals heard a car coming along by The Green and approaching the church. They all tensed and listened intently to hear where it was going.

Then, to their amazement, it slowed down and pulled up outside the churchyard. The burglars were actually parking their car right in front of them! They were cool customers indeed to be so bold as to park their getaway car right in the middle of the village! It was quite possible that the sound of the car, quiet though it was, might disturb someone, who would look out of their window and see them. However, the burglars luck held, as it obviously had throughout their burgling spree, and nothing and no-one stirred in the quiet village.

The animals, hidden in the shadows of the church porch, watched and listened as the couple, dressed completely in black, stealthily got out of the car and walked quietly away in the direction of Mrs Tompkins' house.

Sherpa suddenly appeared at the gate, realised that the waiting animals had seen the car, and set off again, following the two law breakers to their destination. Once there, he found himself a hiding place where he could keep an eye on the house and settled himself comfortably to wait for the couple to reappear. The mission had started!

The couple, young as they were, were obviously skilled at their occupation. No sound, no light came from the house, even though Sherpa's sharp eyes looked hard for signs of the burglars activities.

After twenty minutes Sherpa saw two dark figures creep round the side of the house. He noticed that the man was now carrying a large bag, which he didn't have with him when he left the car. They must have taken a bag from Mrs Tompkins' house to hold all the items they were stealing. How cheeky of them!

With the reappearance of the couple Sherpa melted into the darkness and made his way back to the church. The rest of the gang saw him arrive and met him at the churchyard gate. Carefully pushing the gate open, so as to make as little noise as possible, Brian and Toby slipped out to the pavement outside, while the cats all noiselessly crept over the churchyard wall.

The cats and Toby all found themselves hiding places in the long grass and bushes, while Brian crept round to the driver's side of the car, noticing the rusty dent that Jasper had told them about. He crouched down by the driver's door, determined that no one was going to get into that car while he was on guard!

Two figures suddenly appeared round the corner of the churchyard and made their way quickly towards their car. When they were a few yards from the car Jake suddenly leapt out of his hiding place, yelling, "Now! Now!"

Before the two startled burglars had had time to react to Jake's loud yowl, the silence was broken by the sound of ten yowling cats and two barking dogs.

Toby and the cats danced around the two figures, scratching and nipping at their legs. Beelzebub, returning to the behaviour of his early youth, leapt onto the man's back and dug his claws in hard. Howling in pain, Gerry swung the bag of stolen goods round, in an attempt to dislodge the savage creature hanging on his back, but Beelzebub clung like a limpet.

Melanie kicked at the animals swarming round her, but they were too quick and agile for her. Little Toby dashed in and gave one of her ankles a nasty nip, which caused her, too, to yell out in pain.

Between the yowling of the cats, the barking of the dogs and the agonised yells of the two humans, the noise was deafening. Lights started to go on in bedroom windows and faces were peering out, anxious to see what all the commotion was about.

Then, suddenly, the situation turned serious. Moonlight flashed on something which appeared in Gerry's hand and Libby yelled out, "Look out, he's got a knife! Beelzebub, get down!"

The black cat gave one last swipe at his victim's head, then leapt for safety.

Swinging the knife around to keep the yowling creatures away from him, Gerry ran over to the car. He made his way to the driver's side to be confronted by Brian – the same Brian who had seen off Bozo. Hackles raised, he barked and bared his teeth. Gerry thrust his knife at the angry dog, only for Brian to leap up and take the man's wrist in a vicious grip, his teeth drawing blood. The knife clattered to the floor as Gerry struggled to get away from the dog. Before he had a chance to try to get hold of the knife again, game little Toby dashed forward and picked it up in his mouth, taking it out of range of the vicious thug.

While Gerry was trying desperately to get away from Brian, Melanie was making a determined attempt to save herself. Ignoring Gerry's plight, she waded past the caterwauling cats who were trying to trip her up. Reaching the car, she wrenched the passenger door open, threw herself inside and quickly slammed the door before any of the cats could follow her.

Looking around, she noticed people starting to come out of their houses, most with bemused expressions on their faces. They were trying to work out exactly what was going on.

Melanie felt in her pocket for her house keys and looked on the keyring for the spare car key Gerry had given her. She quickly slid across to the driver's seat, put the key in the ignition and started the car.

Outside, the animals were still creating a caterwauling that hurt people's ears. More and more people from further and further away in the village, were starting to appear in the street asking each other what was going on.

Determined to get away Melanie put her foot on the accelerator and, leaving Gerry to his fate, started to drive off.

As she pulled away up the street a grey blur flew at the car and landed on the windscreen, snarling and hissing at the girl inside. Shocked at the sudden appearance of the apparition in front of her, Melanie yanked the steering wheel to the right in an attempt to dislodge her attacker.

In her haste, however, her foot went down hard on the accelerator and the car shot diagonally across the road and crashed into a tree. The grey blur was catapulted into the air and landed heavily on the pavement, where it lay without moving.

As if a switch had been turned off, as suddenly as it had started the noise stopped abruptly, and both animals and humans stared in horror at the still form lying on the pavement. Ginny, eyes wide with shock, rushed over to where Sherpa lay, her eyes filling with tears.

"Sherpa! Oh, Sherpa!" she whispered. She rubbed her head against him but there was no response.

By now the villagers had begun to realise that the two young people, dressed all in black, had been up to no good and had taken hold of them. Two men held the struggling Gerry, who was swearing and clutching his bleeding hand. Another man was checking on Melanie, who was unhurt but too shocked to make more than a feeble attempt to escape.

The silent animals all made their way over to their fallen comrade. Two women came over and knelt down by Sherpa to see what they could do. One was the local vicar, wearing a rather brightly patterned pair of pyjamas. The other, to the amazement of Jake and his housemates, was Ma, still in her nightie and dressing gown. She and Pa had been woken up by the commotion going on by the churchyard. Finding their animals all missing, they had come looking for them and arrived on the scene in time to see Sherpa's heroic attempt to stop Melanie getting away.

Ma put her hand gently on Sherpa's body but he didn't stir. Ma and the vicar looked at each other anxiously. Then, to the relief of everyone, one eye opened slowly. Sherpa looked blearily at the weeping Ginny and croaked, "It's okay, Girl. Only winded."

There was a collective sigh of sheer relief from all the animals. Then chaos broke out again; dogs and cats barking and yowling in gratitude and villagers all talking at once.

Ginny rubbed her head against Sherpa, saying over and over again, "Oh, Sherpa, my brave Sherpa."

Then, above the noise, the sound of a siren could be heard and, within a minute, a police car appeared with its lights flashing and siren on full blast. The car stopped and the siren went off, although the light continued flashing.

Two policemen got out and, both with expressions of amazement and disbelief, surveyed the scene in front of them; a host of now silent animals, one of which was lying on the pavement, looking rather dazed, as if he'd just done ten rounds with a heavyweight boxer; a large number of people, all apparently in their nightwear; two young people, both bleeding, being held tightly and not particularly happy about it; and finally a car, which looked as if it had been parked up a tree.

The driver of the police car, a sergeant, spoke up. "Which of you phoned the police?"

"I did," said one of the men holding Gerry. "I heard a terrible commotion outside and thought something must be wrong, so I phoned. And I think you'll find these two lovely young people are the burglars you've been looking for."

Both policemen looked at Gerry and Melanie, who were now standing near the car being closely watched by two women, one of whom was brandishing a rather vicious looking umbrella.

Another man, who turned out to be Leo's owner, Marcus Trent, spoke up. "I think it might be a good idea to look inside that bag."

The bag was lying on the ground, where Gerry had dropped it in his efforts to escape his jailers. The policeman said something to his colleague, who returned to the police car and could be seen saying something into the car radio.

The sergeant went over and opened up the bag. Inside was a collection of silver, china and glassware. The sergeant pulled out a large silver cup which, from the inscription, appeared to be first prize in a gardening competition.

The vicar looked up from the pavement, where she was still kneeling by the gradually recovering Sherpa.

"I recognise that cup. Eric Tompkins won that five years ago at a national gardening competition, just before he died. It stands in pride of place on Mary's mantlepiece."

"Is Mrs Tompkins here?" asked the sergeant.

"No," replied the vicar. "I doubt she's even woken up. She sleeps badly and takes sleeping tablets at night."

The second policeman returned and said, "Back up's on its way. DI Franks is coming. He can't wait to get his hands on these two. He's had to put up with so much flack for not catching them before."

"He didn't catch them now," said Marcus Trent, who was perfectly aware of his own cat's presence. "No one would have known anything about them if these animals hadn't been disturbed and made a noise."

Everyone now looked at the little group of animals, who began to feel rather uneasy at being the focus of such attention. Pa, in particular, seemed to be looking very closely at his own cats and dog.

"I think it's time we disappeared," murmured Jake. "We'll get together another time. I'll send a message. Thanks everyone. Great job!"

With that, before anyone could stop them, the animals all melted away in various directions – Sooty and Patch to return to their own village and the rest to their usual nocturnal haunts.

Toby arrived back at his house to find his owner keeping an eye on events outside the churchyard from her front garden. She watched as Toby walked into the garden, with a noticeable bounce in his step, and said suspiciously, "Where've you been? What have you been up to?"

Toby, however, simply trotted past her and made his way into the house through the front door which Mrs Whittacker had left open. He hadn't had so much fun in years!

Jake and his crew, all except Ginny who stayed by Sherpa, made their way quickly back home, closely watched by Pa. When they got home, they found the back door open. In their haste to find their animals Ma and Pa had forgotten to shut it. Brian and the three cats slipped inside and settled on their beds as if they'd never been away.

A few minutes later Ma, Pa and the vicar turned up, Ma carrying Sherpa and the vicar carrying Ginny. Arthur, from next door, was also with them, having met them on his way to investigate the noise coming from the direction of the church. He was a rough, unsentimental man, whose gruff, "What's happened to him?" hid the real affection he had for his cat. Ma, who knew him well, reassured him that Sherpa was unhurt, only winded and possibly bruised in one or two places.

"I'd pop him to the vet on Monday," she said, "just to have him checked over. But I'm sure there's nothing seriously wrong with him. Amazing really."

Arthur carefully took Sherpa from Ma and turned to take him home.

"See you tomorrow, Sherpa?" said Ginny hopefully, but Sherpa, too worn out to say anything, just winked rather weakly at her and was then carried off by Arthur.

"I suppose I'd better go and see where my rascal has got to," said the vicar. "I've a feeling those scratches on that lad's face and head are down to him." With that she gave Ma and Pa a friendly nod and was gone, remembering, with some amusement, the number of times she had had to make excuses for Beelzebub when he was a kitten.

Ma and Pa, left alone with their cats and visitor, looked at the five animals, who looked innocently back at them. Ma's face showed her confusion. How on earth had they got out and how did they come to be involved in the events outside the churchyard?

Pa looked thoughtfully at the animals. He was beginning to think that his suspicions about their activities were not so far from the truth. He had recognised Mangy Tom as the stray Libby had brought to dinner a couple of times. His rather disturbing thoughts were interrupted by Ma saying, "What do you think happened Pa? Do you think the noise disturbed them and they went to see what it was? Although I can't think how they got out."

"Yes," agreed Pa. "That's probably what happened."

But he no more believed that than he believed the moon was made of cheese. His common sense told him that cats and dogs couldn't communicate and plan and organise. Nevertheless, he looked at the five innocent faces looking up at him, Brian's still with a smear of blood on his muzzle, and he wondered. Eventually he took a deep breath and said, "Come on, back to bed. Excitement over."

They locked the back door and then made their way upstairs, with Ma saying, "We've got to search the house until we find out how they got out."

"Tomorrow!" said Pa, firmly. "When we get up, we'll have a good look round and see what we can find."

He really didn't fancy any more surprises at the moment. He could almost believe that they would find a set of keys tucked under one of the cat's beds!

Once Ma and Pa had gone, the five animals looked at each other gleefully.

"We did it!" said Jake, jubilantly. "Those two young tearaways have been caught red handed."

"In more ways than one!" laughed Libby, looking meaningfully at Brian.

"Gerry deserved it," said Wesley. "Threatening Brian with a knife. You were very brave, Brian." He looked at Ginny. "And so was Sherpa."

"You see what 'only cats' can do when they put their minds to it?" Jake said.

"Not to mention, 'only dogs'!" added Wesley. "In future those words are banned from this house."

Libby rubbed her head against Jake. "I really didn't think we would do it."

"I'm not really sure that I did either," admitted Jake. Then he looked round at the others and added proudly, "But we had a good team and our last-minute member turned out to be a real asset. Did you see him go for Melanie's ankles?" They all laughed.

"What do you think is going on back at the churchyard?" wondered Wesley. "I wish we could have stayed to see what happened."

Jake shook his head. "It was better not to. I'm sure we'll hear all about it tomorrow, one way or another. Come on let's get some sleep now."

The animals all curled up on their beds, tired but triumphant and, in Brian's case, more than a little amazed at himself.

Chapter Thirteen

Ma and Pa were up early that morning, despite the excitement of the night, in order to have a good look for the animals escape route before they went to church. It didn't take them long to find the open study window. Pa got a telling off from Ma for his carelessness in leaving the window open.

"If I've told you once I've told you a dozen times to make sure you shut and lock that window," scolded Ma, but in a tone that was far less cross than might have been expected.

"I know, I know, I'm sorry. It won't happen again."

For some reason Pa was happily taking the blame, even though he knew perfectly well that he had last been in the study nearly a fortnight ago and the window had been firmly shut then, due to the fact that it was pouring with rain.

He sat down at the breakfast table but as he ate his food and drank his tea, his eyes were repeatedly drawn to the five innocent looking animals, who eventually began to feel uneasy at his puzzled interest in them.

"Why is he looking at us like that?" asked Brian.

The cats all shook their heads. Then Libby suggested, "He might be wondering how we got the window open. He'll know it would have been closed."

"Why didn't he tell Ma that it wasn't him?" Wesley asked the question they were all thinking. They all looked back at Pa with the same puzzled look he was giving them. Eventually Pa went back to his breakfast and the animals relaxed again.

After giving the animals their breakfast, Ma and Pa left for church. They were occasional churchgoers, but Ma felt it would be a good idea to go on this particular Sunday. Pa didn't question why, he knew!

They were gone for much longer than they usually were. When they finally arrived back home it was clear that most of the village had suddenly felt the need to go to church that morning. The vicar, a sensible woman, had kept her sermon short, knowing that all her congregation wanted to do was to discuss the events that had taken place only a few hours before.

It seemed that those who had been present took centre stage, filling in the unfortunate people who had missed out. Mrs Tompkins, as the burglars' victim, was treated with great interest, even though she had slept through the whole thing. In spite of having her belongings stolen, she was thoroughly enjoying being the centre of attention.

When Ma and Pa got home, Pa went off to the snug to read the Sunday papers and Ma phoned Mad Mary to tell her all about it, which was how the animals learnt what had happened after they had made themselves scarce.

It had taken the two policemen some time to get everyone to calm down so that they could find out exactly what had happened. A second police car had arrived with the DI, who had arrested Gerry and Melanie, and they had been handcuffed and taken away to the police station in the two cars.

It seemed that DI Franks had recognised Gerry – it wasn't the first time he had been arrested for breaking into people's houses. The police had searched his flat, which was in the nearby town of Littlebury, not in one of the villages, and found all the stolen items from the previous burglaries.

Telling the villagers that they would be back later to take statements, the police left and the villagers rather reluctantly returned to their homes. Like Toby, they hadn't had so much excitement for years.

It was clear that the villagers felt the animals had been instrumental in catching the burglars, but also obvious that they felt the animals' presence was coincidental and their actions the result of being frightened or annoyed by the couple. The cats felt it was a pity they would get no credit for planning the whole thing, but at least now they knew exactly what they could achieve when they really put their minds to it.

Ma's phone call to her sister lasted nearly an hour, with Mad Mary being thrilled to get a blow-by-blow account from someone who had actually been there. If Ma was surprised that the animals stayed put in the kitchen, ignoring the open back door, it would never have occurred to her that they too, were listening to the information she was giving Mad Mary!

They were glad they had stayed because at the end of the phone call Ma invited her sister over for lunch the next day, which almost certainly meant that Max would be coming too.

"Great!" said Jake, jubilantly. "We can arrange our get together with the Spy Club members for tomorrow now."

"Isn't it going to be a bit short notice?" said Wesley, adding cheekily, "The 'Spy Club' members might not be available."

"We'll get Mangy Tom to let them all know. They'll all turn up. You'll see."

"How do we know we'll see him in time?" asked Libby. "We don't know when he'll be around."

Jake grinned. "He'll be here today, I bet you anything."

And he was right.

When Ma had finished her phone call and there was nothing more for the animals to learn, they wandered up the garden to the apple tree and there, on the back wall, was Mangy Tom.

"Happened to be this way," he said casually, "so I thought I'd call in. See how Sherpa is."

"We're glad to see you," said Jake. "Thanks for your help last night."

Tom nodded his head in response. He didn't often get thanked for things. His actions usually meant he had a shoe or something similar thrown at him!

Jake went on to tell Tom about the planned meeting the next day and he offered, not only to speak to the cats in the other villages, but to see Leo and Beelzebub as well.

"Don't forget Toby," said Brian.

Mangy Tom nodded. "No problem, but I'll have to find somewhere to get something to eat first."

Libby, taking the hint, took him down to the kitchen where Ma, recognising him, gave him a plate of food. The other animals managed to resist making any comments about

Libby's 'conquest' for fear of annoying Tom, and Pa, who was safely in the snug, was not there to notice the presence yet again of the black and white stray.

Once Tom had left, the animals settled under the apple tree to go over their triumph yet again, until Ma called them in for their tea.

While they were eating their tea, the phone rang. Claire was phoning from the hotel in Dubai. Ma assured her that Brian was fine but decided that an account of the night's adventures could wait until Claire was home. She merely told Claire to enjoy her holiday, said goodbye and then went round the house, checking that all doors and windows were firmly locked, before going upstairs to bed.

Chapter Fourteen

The following morning two policemen came to take statements from Ma and Pa but, as they all went into the sitting room, the animals couldn't hear what was being said.

When they came into the kitchen again one of the policemen grinned and said, "So are these some of the burglar busting animals, then?"

All five animals, particularly Brian, managed to look totally half-witted and the second policeman laughed. "They don't look like a crime busting gang to me."

The four humans laughed, Pa somewhat weakly, and then the policemen left, having thanked Ma and Pa for their help. The animals followed them out of the back door and made their way up to the top of the garden.

Shortly after the policemen had left Mad Mary and Max arrived. Mad Mary, having seen the police car drive off, was rather peeved to have missed the policemen, but went into the kitchen with Ma demanding that she told her the whole story again.

Max made his way up to the apple tree, well aware that the others were anxiously awaiting his arrival. He sat down slowly, then looked around at the eager faces looking back at him and smiled.

"So, you succeeded in your enterprise little brother. Well done, all of you." Then he added, half seriously and half-jokingly, "You seem to have gathered yourself an efficient network of spies."

Jake bridled with pride at this unusual praise from his older brother, but said, "We couldn't have done it without you, Max. The information you got from Bruiser was invaluable. Please give him our thanks. It was a joint effort; everyone played a part."

Feeling satisfied that his work had been acknowledged, Max relaxed and said kindly, "Well come on, tell me all about it."

They needed no further encouragement and launched into a babble of information which Max just about managed to understand. To be truthful, he felt just a little bit sorry that he hadn't been involved himself, although he would never have admitted it!

To everyone's joy and relief, just before lunchtime, Sherpa appeared through the gap in the hedge, walking rather stiffly but grinning with satisfaction. He nodded at Max and then sat down by Ginny, who licked him once or twice and then sat gazing adoringly at him.

"Well, who's the hero of the hour?" asked Jake, who seemed to have completely forgotten that the 'hero of the hour' was a 'common farm cat'.

Sherpa looked round and said modestly, "Seems to me there were a lot of heroes. I imagine both Gerry and Melanie have bites and scratches which will take some time to heal."

It turned out that Sherpa himself had had a visit to the vet that morning, with Arthur being concerned enough to take Ma's advice. The vet had said he was fine and that any stiffness would soon wear off.

Before they had a chance to discuss anything more, Mangy Tom appeared on the back wall.

"Messages delivered. Sooty and Patch will be here, Jasper said to say hello and also Lucy Locket and Fred, who are looking forward to meeting you all. Fluffball and Barney can't come but both said any time you need information they'd be glad to help." Having run out of breath, Mangy Tom stopped for a second and then continued. "Saw Leo. He said he'd see Beelzebub and Toby. Should be a nice little reunion."

The little group of animals settled down to wait for their visitors, half wondering if any of them would turn up. But sure enough, early in the afternoon Sooty and Patch appeared, closely followed by Leo and Beelzebub. All the visiting cats hid themselves in the greenery near to the apple tree, so as not to draw the attention of the humans.

Then two strange cats, a longhaired tortoiseshell and a brown tabby, who appeared through the bushes bordering the house on the other side of the garden to Sherpa's, turned out to be Lucy Locket and Fred. Introductions were made and then the two newcomers joined the other visitors in the undergrowth.

Finally, perky little Toby appeared at the gateway to the house and, bold as brass, trotted up the garden and sat down by Brian – feeling that there were an awful lot of cats around. Everyone looked at their hosts as if to say, "Well, we're here. What now?"

Max turned to Jake, "This was your idea. It's up to you."

Jake glanced round and then started to speak. "First of all, thanks to all of you. We couldn't have done it without you." He looked at Wesley. "As we said to ourselves last night, it just shows what we cats and dogs can do when we put our minds to it. Between us we caught a very nasty pair of crooks." Then he looked at Brian. "And I want to apologise to you, Brian." Brian's mouth fell open. What was coming now? Was Jake about to make one of his sarcastic comments? "We haven't always been very nice to you and called you a wimp," continued Jake. "Well, we were wrong and we won't make that mistake again. You're a demon when you're roused."

Everyone laughed and Sherpa added, "I think Gerry would agree with that!" and everyone laughed again. Brian felt that life just couldn't get any better.

"You too, Sherpa," continued Jake. "You really showed us just what a *mere farm cat* can do. You were incredibly brave."

Sherpa looked at Jake with a very serious expression on his face. Then he grinned. "With my brawn and your brains, we'll make a formidable duo." He paused and looked around. "Is this the end then?"

"What do you mean?" asked Jake, frowning.

"Is this the one and only adventure that Jake's Spy Club is going to have?"

"Well, Max said we've set up an efficient network of spies. We'll be ready the next time we're needed."

Beelzebub interrupted. "I hope we don't have too many crimes here. The vicar wouldn't like it."

Once again, the little gang broke into laughter and then, all feeling a great sense of satisfaction, began discussing the events of the past few days; some of the newcomers hearing for the first time of the home cats' adventures with Bozo and the two cruel boys.

Libby sat back and listened, looking approvingly at Jake, who was making no attempt to monopolise the conversation. It must have cost him a lot to make those apologies to Brian and Sherpa, especially in front of all the other animals. He would make a good leader for his little Spy Club.

Eventually, as afternoon became early evening, the visitors began drifting away, promising to keep the communication lines open. Mad Mary appeared at the back door calling Max to go back home and Sherpa disappeared through the gap in the hedge, deciding that he'd have a night at home with Arthur for once. Brian and the four cats stayed happily under the apple tree soaking up the last rays of the summer sun and all feeling contented with life.

None of the animals had any idea that Pa's sharp eyes had seen the cats hiding in the undergrowth. He had recognised several from the group at the churchyard and he watched the little gang closely. He knew, like the intelligent man that he was, that their appearance at the church had been accidental, their behaviour the result of fear. But, for all his intelligence, amazing and unbelievable as it was, it looked to him as if the little group of animals was having a meeting. So, Pa watched and wondered. Oh yes, he wondered very much.